THE OLD DOG

THE OLD DOG

A WESTERN DOUBLE

LEVI JOHNSON MOUNTAIN MAN SCOUT

BOOK FIVE

ASH LINGAM

WOLFPACK
PUBLISHING
— EST 2013 —

CONTENTS

THE OLD DOG

UNFORGOTTEN

THE OLD DOG

THE OLD DOG

LEVI JOHNSON MOUNTAIN MAN SCOUT 9

This book is dedicated to my Malinois dog, Lola.

"I shall live badly if I don't write,
and I will write badly if I don't live."

Francoise Sagan

WOLVES & DOGS

THE OLD DOG WAS SCARRED AND HAD ONE CLOUDY EYE, but that didn't deter him from a fight—something he had been doing since the beginning of his existence. His sense of smell and hearing made up for his vision loss on one side. Four wolves circled the old wild canine as his ears and tail pointed straight up. The hair on its back stood on end from its ears to its rump. The dog stood its ground, knowing that if it ran, it would bolster the wolves' courage, and they might all attack at once. He had no intention of giving up a meal anyway, so there he stood with the odds against him again.

This wasn't the first dance for the apparently ageless animal. Its massive body was covered in healed wounds, and it was missing two of its lower front teeth. But the large canine incisors shone white in the limited light of dusk. This was the time for predators to come out and begin their nightly hunt for nourishment and to fight for their territories. The four wolves intended to do both.

The dog sensed it was in the wolf's territory well

before he saw them, but he didn't stray from his intended path for anything, even a pack of ravenous killers. In the middle of the hungry pack was a downed doe. Their muzzles were sticky and red from their prey, but the hungry old dog wasn't backing down. Little did the predators know this dog could fight like thunder and was as quick as lightning.

The animal instinctively knew it wasn't the size of the dog in the fight—it was the size of the fight in the dog. The ancient canine became very rigid and still. Its guttural growling sounded threatening even though it was facing four opponents. It lunged forward, just short of contact. It appeared to be waiting for some sign of weakness or movement that would make one or more vulnerable to its massive jaws.

The dog had been in so many battles during its lifetime that it no longer feared anything in the forest. Only the grizzly was fiercer in it, but the dog was still faster than the bear. It wouldn't be a squabble; it would be for the prize, so at least one of the five four-legged animals there would die, if not more. The wolves before him were threatened with displays of growling, snapping, snarling, and biting at each other; still, their instinct told them to keep their distance. The dog was old—it must have arrived at such a ripe age for a reason.

Although its enemies were contentious, the old dog was pugnacious and combative. Finally, the aging canine stood stiff and crouched, leaning his body's position, ready to lunge. With ears up and tail at twelve o'clock, its pupils dilated as it barked and growled. It was ready for the brawl. The wolves acted out of fear, making them aggressive and territorial. The dog's aggression was idiopathic. It wasn't your average Indian camp dog found across the mountains. It was enormous. When the attack came, it went for its opponents' soft stomachs, throats, and front legs. Its massive jaws could snap a wolf's leg like a twig.

Two wolves would feed on the carcass as the other two fended off the trespassing canine. As their level of excitement increased, they snapped at each other as they neared a frenzy.

The dog's ears twitched when it heard the metal click, but it knew if it turned its back on the wolves, they might be the ones tearing at his soft underbelly. The gunshot—a growling wolf was slung ten feet like a rag doll, and its companions scattered. The old dog spun on its hind feet and faced the new threat. It stood its ground despite the danger of the gun. It knew instantly it was a human. He could smell him before he shot.

Rusty Steel grinned at the mongrel. It was nearly as shaggy and as the aging mountain man. He liked how he stood up to the wolves and even stood up to him. It made him chuckle because it reminded him of himself. He wondered where it came from. It was the largest dog he had ever seen. Perhaps it was a breed indigenous to the mountains. Maybe Angus or Dennis could shine some light on the mystery. He felt an instant attraction to the canine, unlike most humans he met, whether they were red, black, or white.

"You look like a tough old cob, just like me." Rusty grinned. "You sure are a big old fella."

The dog tilted its head, staring at the hairy man, and stopped growling. It opened its mouth and panted as its tongue hung out. It didn't sense fear or aggression like it did with the wolves or other humans. It sniffed the air and twitched its ears, then turned its back on Rusty and began to feed on the deer the wolves had killed. He sat where he stood and watched.

He had left his mule a way back, tied to a tree. It was far enough away that the wild animals wouldn't hear it and close enough to keep the predators away with his rifle. He had been hunting for elk but found the wolves instead. He had tracked them to the dead deer. He hadn't even seen the dog's tracks. He wondered how that was.

When the tough old animal had its fill, it walked over to Rusty and curled beside him, sitting on a blanket. It closed its eyes and fell asleep in the snow; minutes later, it snored lightly. The mountain man's face showed his surprise, but there was a satisfaction there too. He dared to stroke its head, and rather than snapping out at the strange man's hand, it sighed a relaxing breath. It apparently had no fear of the mountain man —especially the one who had just saved him from a terrible fight with the pack of wolves.

Rusty wondered who would have won—the apparently aging dog or the wolves. He felt the old dog had been around for some time, and he had become accustomed to fighting off killer wolves. It was that or starve or, even worse—become the pack's next meal.

He pulled a stale biscuit from his pocket and munched as he sat and waited. He wanted to see what the dog would do when he woke up, and the human was still there, but it continued to sleep. It appeared entirely at rest and calm. Rusty carefully stood—the dog opened one eye to see what he was doing, then went back to sleep. Meanwhile, Steel skinned the dead wolf for its fur. When he was done, he looked around and found the dog was gone. Rusty's heart sank.

He built a fire in the last vestiges of light and sat and stared into the flames. It was a shame the dog had run off, but that seemed to be his life story. Nothing ever appeared to be what it really was. He watched as the flames cast dancing shadows on the trees surrounding him. He slept close to the fire as now the temperatures at night dripped well below freezing. But he had a bearskin bedroll and used his fur coat as additional cover. Only his breath was visible under all that hair.

Steel thought he had found a new friend, but it was only his shadow. All that was left was the imprint where it curled up to sleep. At least that proved it had been there, and he knew it wasn't just his imagination. He wondered where it went. It probably went back from to where it came from.

The following day, Rusty rolled the bloody fur up and carried it to his hobbled mule. His mountain lion claw necklace clicked as he walked. Rusty's knee-high moccasins crunched the ice-covered snow with each step. When he got to his mule, he saw its breath. It was standing beside a sleeping dog. Somehow it had smelled the animal of burden and waited for the human.

"Does this mean we be friends and you're not just my shadow, old fella?" Rusty asked.

The dog lifted its head and tilted it to one side like it questioned the human. When he untied his mule, who didn't appear to fear the massive beast either, it stood and wagged its tail. Rusty smiled. He didn't know what it was, but there was something so familiar about the dog that he felt he had known it for years when they had only just met.

"I reckon it's time we headed back home, Dog,"

Rusty said. "You take well enough to me, but how will ya take to strangers?"

The canine's head was massive, and its long legs carried a large-chested body. It had long, shaggy hair and was as black as coal. Somehow, the mountain man felt that he and the dog were never strangers. How this was, he didn't know, and he imagined that the dog didn't either. Some things were just meant to be and were often difficult to explain. He had learned this time and again over the years. It had always been the same for him, from when he was a small child living in the streets and harbor of St. Luis.

They carefully walked through the wilderness, both man and beast seeking out danger. The dog walked with its nose to the ground and ears alert. It sniffed the snow-covered trail as it raced forward. Sometimes it disappeared out of sight, and Rusty wondered if it would return or not. It was obviously a free spirit. Despite its ancient appearance, it seemed as fit and agile as a young pup. At times it was almost playful, but Rusty didn't know his new friend that well yet. He was aware those massive jaws could break his arm and rip out his throat, but he felt no ill will from the animal.

The next night when they camped, the dog waited on supper. It stared fixed at Rusty as he made up a pot of salted pork and beans. He filled a pan for his new friend, and it ate the plate clean in seconds. His long tongue lapped the last bean from the pie pan. Then it licked its lips and stared some more at his newfound human.

"It don't look like you got enough to eat with that deer, did ya, boy," Rusty said. "I reckon you'll eat me out of house and home. I just hope you take kindly to the other folks that live in the cabin with us and don't take a mind to eat 'im."

The dog looked at the human questioningly. It seemed to raise its brow. There was something uncanny about the animal. It was far more intelligent than any canine the mountain man had ever seen. It appeared to be one-of-a-kind.

Once they had returned from rescuing Levi and Forrester with the Crow Indians, Rusty felt he needed some time alone, so he took a short journey into the winter snow. He didn't do it to search for beaver pelts, though. He was out hunting and checking out the winter's progress on their mountain.

Suppose he found a large elk that was fine too. They could always use the hide, and the meat was delicious. It was the favorite of all the mountain men and most Indians. But he had left just to get away on his own. Maybe he was a little jealous of the journey the two you men had taken. He knew he was getting on in years. He was almost fifty, and in these parts, that was nearly an old man.

Many men meet their maker in the wilderness well before they turn the ripe age of a half century. Rusty figured he had another decade in him if Mother Nature permitted. In the wilderness, the mountain men lived from one day to the next because they never knew what tomorrow would bring.

A New Home

When Dahteste arrived with Levi and company at the compound, they stayed in Angus and Rusty's cabin for the first days. But the Crow war chief insisted on having their own home—something more like what she was used to. The old mountain men sent up smoke signals as instructed by Dahteste. Two days later, three horses arrived dragging travois with supplies to build a tipi for her and Johnson to live in. By then, they had cut long pine poles for the frame. It was covered in hides and even had a rolling door and smoke ventilator with a flap.

Flames flashed over burning coals in the center of the lodge giving everything inside an orange tint. The floor was covered in thick bear skins, as was their bed. Levi expected it to take some getting used to, but his feelings for Dahteste were enough to make everything bearable. Their tipi was set up between Dennis's and Rusty's cabins. The lodge was assembled in a few days after the mountain men cut and cleaned the poles. Everybody joined in and lent a helping hand to the newcomer to the compound. In what seemed impossible, a comfortable Indian home was constructed between Mountain Dennis's cabin and Rusty Steel's in only days.

Dahteste was so pretty that all the mountain men fell head over heels to help her in any way they could, and all of them were envious of Levi—everybody but the captain. He was still struggling with who he was and who he wasn't. He seemed to be in constant change. One day he thought he knew what he wanted out of life, and the next, it seemed to be something different.

Considering Forrester was the most intelligent and educated man on the mountain, he had little idea about what he wanted to do and where he would end up. He wanted to be a mountain man and achieved just that even though he lost an arm learning. Now he had shaved off his beard and was acting more like a soldier than a frontiersman again. Time would tell what he decided what he really wanted to do or who he really was.

One thing Will knew for sure—he couldn't return to Orange County, New York. His West Point peers would have him for breakfast after losing the expedition. All his friends knew it was something he would have to work out on his own, just like when he lost his arm. Some things a man had to find himself without any help from outside, so they all gave him his space. Now that Beaver Johnson didn't have time for his friend with his new life, he seemed like a rudderless ship on some distant sea. It was going to take some getting used to. He wondered if he would run aground or sink before that.

"And here I thought I was gonna have to build

another cabin for us next spring," Levi said in Crow, grinning from ear to ear.

"White men make their homes to last for many years," Dahteste said, "but what happens when the buffalo or elk move to another part of the mountain? Even the big Crow camp I come from can be moved to another location in a week. We have already lived in several places, and I'm still young. The Plains Indians have roamed after our food and shelter for thousands of years. Where the buffalo go, we follow. We don't need to spend half a year to make something we can make in a few days. Don't you feel cozy here in our warm tipi?"

"I reckon I never thought of having a cabin like that," Levi pondered. "It, sure enough, wouldn't be able to take it with us if we had to move. We come up here to get away from people and something we call civilization. Then again, our streams are getting' trapped out, and Rusty says the wild game is scarcer than it was just a short while ago."

"Civilization?" Dahteste asked. "In my camp, we are many. I doubt this thing you call civilization will reach us here in the sacred mountains. Only when the Rendezvous comes are there white, black, and even yellow men here to buy and sell their wares. Each year come more too. Is that what you mean? They only stay here for two weeks or so. It gives the local Indians a chance to trade beaver pelts for tools and coffee. The meet is as important for the local Indians as it is for the trappers."

"Maybe you don't see it now, but civilization is comin', and there ain't nobody's gonna be able to stop it," Johnson said. "I thought you told me we would work on your English."

"I am—working on English," Dahteste said in English and smiled, then reverted to Crow. "But today, we will work on our tipi and your Crow. When I take you to meet my family, I don't want you to speak like a child."

"Speakin' like a youngin' is a danged sight better than not speakin' any Indian at all," Levi laughed. "I thought you didn't wanna go back because of what happened to your war party. It's a hard thing to lose your men. I seen what it done to Forrester. It tore him up, and it's still eatin' away at him like a couple of rats gnawing at his insides."

"That was before someone other than me disclosed what really happened to my war party," Dahteste replied. "If I had returned alone without my men, it would have been a disgrace. I was saved by pure chance, just like you and the captain. I survived because it was my destiny. One day we will go to my home and spend some time. Maybe a month or two, and you can perfect your Crow. I am sure I will learn fast with all eight of you speaking English. I also speak some Blackfoot and Ute."

"Why would you learn the languages of your enemies?" Levi asked.

"The better you know your enemy, the more chance you will have to lead your war party to victory," Dahteste said. "I believe that now I better learn English."

"I hope you don't look at us as the enemy," Johnson huffed. "Still, you know as well as I do that some White men are our enemies, too, like the scalpers. A good part of the folks that come west is runnin' away from somethin' or somebody. A good dose of 'im is runnin' from the law."

"I would never see you as a danger to me," Dahteste said. Her eyes pooled. "You saved me," she added in a whisper. Her eyes coaxed him to come to her.

"Let's get back under the covers," Dahteste said with dreamy eyes. She was cuddled up with the furry bearskin wrapped in her arms and against her chin. She blinked her large brown eyes.

"But we just got up, darlin'," Levi replied, smiling. "We can have a siesta later."

"Maybe Pine Needle will bring Angus to the Crow camp when I take you to meet my family," Dahteste said. "Then you won't feel so strange at first."

"Did you know Angus before?" Levi asked.

"No, but I know Pine Needle. She is a friend of my mother. Our camp is big, but I know most of our tribe. I know them on sight if I don't know them by name."

"There must be five hundred people in your camp. At least, that's what Forrester said."

"The captain is a very clever man." Dahteste smiled. "You can see by the way he walks he was trained to be a White warrior."

"Why do you call Forrester the captain?" Levi asked. "Will Forrester, I mean. I told ya he wasn't in the United States Army anymore."

"Does a warrior stop being a warrior because he leaves his camp?" Dahteste asked. "You can tell he is a soldier no matter how he dressed. Especially when he carries his long sword."

"His saber?" Levi huffed. "Is that why you think he still be a captain? I always said carryin' that thing around would come to no good one day, but the man knows how to wield it. I've seen him lob a man's head clean off with one slice. It's so sharp you can drop an apple on the blade, and it'll cut it clean in two."

"And the horse?" Dahteste added. "Do normal men ride war horses? You can see it in his eyes too. He also shaves, and you other men don't. He is intentionally different. He even treats his missing arm like a battle trophy."

"Now that you say it all that way, I reckon you're right," Levi said, scratching his head thoughtfully. "Actually, I always see him as a captain, too, but then again, I was his scout back in Kansas."

"You were an army scout?" Dahteste asked, surprised. "You seem too wild for the army. You are more like an Indian than your friend Forrester. He will always be a captain, even if he doesn't seem to know it. It is in his blood like being a war chief is in my blood."

"Yeah, but he had a couple of real bad run-ins with the Comanche," Johnson said. "They nearly wiped us out. They killed more than half the folks in our expedition. I reckon the captain's got some of that guilt you live with as a war chief. I reckon it's pretty much the same, ain't it."

"Comanche," Dahteste whispered. "I have never fought them but hear many songs and stories. They are the most dreaded of all the enemies, and we have plenty. Most tribes fight over land, much like White men."

"Yeah, but the only difference there is the White folks want all the land and ain't happy with just part of it like your folks, the Blackfeet and the Ute," Levi warned. "That's something that seems to be in our nature for the most part. We're a greedy lot; we are."

"How does it feel to have such a woman as me?"

Dahteste asked, "Do White women become captains too?"

"Not that I know of." Levi laughed. "Not yet anyway. I reckon enough women fight their way across the wilderness, though. That ought to count for somethin'. I figure you Indians be a jump ahead of White folks on that. Maybe one day, women will have a bigger part in things. You've got to admit, without 'im, there's a lot of lonely men. I've read that women only represent ten percent of the White population west of the Missouri River."

"There is no shortage of Crow Indian women." Dahteste smiled, and it reached her sparkling eyes. "Maybe one day Forrester will find a woman. Perhaps a Crow woman warrior like me." She laughed, transforming her face and making her more beautiful than ever.

"I don't rightly know if the captain and a woman warrior could live under the same roof without killin' each other." Levi chuckled. "He'd be better off with a normal wife, even if she is Crow. At the moment, he's still figuring himself out. That's something he appears to do every little bit. He sure as heck wasn't cut out to carry the weight of his dead soldiers on his shoulders. At least not, unless he learns to be thicker-skinned. He takes it all to heart when runnin' it over and over in his mind don't do anybody any good."

Dahteste raked her fingers through Levi's beard and said, "Indians rarely have beards and never thick like you. I like to feel it on my face. It tickles my nose."

Heat came in waves from the fire as smoke squirreled up and out the vent. The floor was deep in layers of furs. Dahteste made them breakfast. Since Hachta had been trading tobacco, coffee, and steel tools with Rusty Steel and the mountain men, most Indians drank coffee when they could. Of course, she had Levi's part of the supplies he hunted most of anyway. He was the head hunter of the compound and brought in twice that of the rest combined. His trapping and hunting skills were now second to none.

"We're gonna have to go out huntin' together." Levi smiled. He never thought he would find a woman so much like himself. Dahteste fit him right down to his boots. "Woo to the fella that crosses our paths." He laughed until he got a stitch as his woman beamed.

MOUNTAIN LIONS

As Rusty Steel and his new friend, Dog, continued through the forest on their way back to the compound, they hunted as they went. The dog seemed to be a natural and ran ahead of his master with its nose glued to the ground. It would occasionally look back with snow piled on its snout and its legs up to its chest in drifts. They had seen the tracks quickly enough. It was nearly impossible not to see them, but they disappeared suddenly without a trace of where the large cat had gone. That was when Dog began to sniff the tree beside the trail and barked like it had treed a raccoon.

Massive tracks were visible in the snow up to a point. Rusty stretched his hand across the pawprint, and it was much bigger. He shook his head and looked around. He sniffed the air but nothing. Dog dropped its head and began to growl from deep inside.

Icy wind peppered his rosy cheeks as he pulled his cap down over his ears to keep them from freezing. Both Rusty and the dog's breath vanished right after it appeared. The sun reflected off the snow making the human squint the light out. Everywhere he looked was white snow as far as the eye could see. Half the earth was white, and the other half sky-blue.

Rusty looked up at the limbs and foliage overhead. He didn't dare walk under the mountain lion giving it a chance to pounce on his head. He pulled back the large hammer on his long rifle—the click sounded loud in the silence. He traced the barrel along the trees overhead, staring down the sight. Dog ran ahead, and in less than a minute, he began to bark again. Steel slowly crept forward toward the sound of his new animal friend. When he got there, he saw Dog was after a new set of tracks where the cat leaped from tree to tree and finally back down to the ground.

That told Rusty it knew they were following it, which made it all the more dangerous. The paws were massive—as big as any cats he had ever seen. It gave him pause, and he stopped for a moment. He wondered if he still had the stuff it took to take on one of the kings of the forest. It could be more dangerous than even a grizzly bear. This was an enormous cat, and it wouldn't hesitate to kill the dog, not alone the human being.

The mountain man and the dog crept through the forest, ever aware that the cat knew precisely where they were, and they hadn't even caught sight of the animal yet. Rusty followed Dog as it moved forward close to the ground, ready to leap at the prey at any moment. He wondered if the wild cat was larger than his new friend. He knew he had to shoot the savage animal before it had time to turn on them both. He listened for sounds but nothing, yet his dog's ears twitched and turned like sunflowers turn to the sun.

The hardened top layer of snow crunched under his

snowshoes. He continued to follow the tracks until again they suddenly vanished. This time the mountain lion seemed to disappear into thin air. They were above the tree line; only rocks and stones hid under the snow. Levi sprouted hackles on his neck as his breathing quickened along with his heart. It pounded loud between his ears as he listened as hard as he could for any sound of the big cat.

"Maybe he's run off after all, old boy," Rusty said, patting the dog's head. "I reckon he was scared of such a big old hound." He chuckled at his paranoia. He had lived in the mountains for years and always held his own, and he didn't plan to start backing down now.

They continued to climb up a steep cliff. Dog had his nose in the snow sniffing for the smell of the cat they were pursuing. It seemed to keep just far enough ahead of them to keep them from catching sight of the threat, but they knew exactly what it was. Rusty's heart beat so loudly that he worried the mountain lion would hear.

"We best get this animal taken care of before it gets dark, Dog," Rusty said. "If not, he's gonna take us out at night. You may be able to see 'im, but I ain't gonna be able to see a thing, not alone shoot it. I doubt a big fire would run it off."

That was when Dog started a low grumble from deep in its chest. It rumbled like a small earthquake until it grew and grew. It sounded like it was far away at first, but then it became louder and louder until it was a roar. Dog spun around, facing Rusty showing bright white fangs as it snarled, and drool dripped from its mouth. It puffed out its chest and roared louder.

That was when he realized they weren't chasing the cat anymore—the mountain lion was now tracking them, and if he wasn't quick, they would be its dinner. Rusty spun on his heels as he swung the gun barrel around. By the time he saw the cat, he was too late, though. The long rifle was too heavy to move quickly enough. He watched as the tan-colored cat dropped from above—its legs spread wide, its paws open, its claws extended, and its wild animal eyes staring down.

Everything seemed to go into slow motion. At first, the lion looked little because it hid high on the cliff. As it fell, it grew bigger and bigger until it blocked out the light. Rusty went down with the cat but tossed his rifle clear and grabbed his large knife. He slashed at the animal on top of him. The impact was bone-crushing even though the cat landed on its feet. As he fought, he struggled to catch his breath. He had the wind knocked out of him, making him struggle harder. His face turned red.

It was a beast, but he was an Indian fighter and trapper, so they tumbled in the dirt as they wrestled for their lives; he wasn't about to give up. Sharp claws appeared between the fingers in its paws. Rusty felt they were razor sharp as they sliced a filet down his face. Blood poured from the wound, but it was cut so clean it didn't even hurt—at least not yet while in the heat of the battle.

The sheer weight of the cat pinned him down, but he stabbed at the side of the mass of muscle and fur until his knife was bloody—but the cat didn't appear to be affected by the wounds. The lion managed to swing a giant paw and caught the mountain man in the temple. His head spun, and he nearly lost consciousness, but he managed to shake it off, blinking his eyes. He gobbled up a little more air as his heart felt like it would burst out of his chest.

The cat roared—Rusty could feel its wet breath on his face. That was when he saw the dog out of the corner of his eye as it ran for the mountain lion with its jaws open. Saliva dripped from its canine teeth. It closed in on the struggling human who was just about to lose the fight. The look in its black eyes was wild and savage, and it showed no fear. Both its ears and tail were pointed at twelve o'clock, and its hair ruffled all along its back.

In the final leap, it launched itself into the air, but the mountain lion was busy with the fight with Rusty. It didn't even see the ball of muscle and teeth coming. The dog hit the mountain lion so hard Rusty heard ribs crack. Like a flash, it had its teeth wrapped around the cat's face. Instantly it was off the man and turned its fury at the dog. Blood poured from the jagged tears in the cat's head, but it swatted its paws with claws extended just the same. It was in a death grip, but it knew the tables might turn if it could break it.

When the canines sank into the cat's eye, it screamed like a dying woman. The eye popped like a fish egg and ran down the lion's face. The bone around its eye cracked loud. Now rather than trying to kill the dog, it had suddenly changed its intentions, and all it wanted to do was escape, but that wasn't in the cards. Dog planned to make his dinner from the mountain lion. It had tasted its blood, and now the thirst for death was intuitive and impossible to stop.

The cat's mouth was trapped between the giant jaws as it struggled to breathe, trying to get one last gasp of air. It kicked and wiggled frantically, but the dog held it firm in its teeth. It used its mouth to push the cat's body flat on the ground as the canine held it in its vise-like jaws. Finally, it ended, and the cat fell limp on the ground.

The dog let go of its head and sniffed the dear prey. He wanted to make sure it was dead. It tore at the soft underbelly and had its fill. When it looked up and locked eyes with Rusty, its muzzle was covered in blood. He suddenly realized this dog was more a wild animal than a pet. He wondered if it would have him for supper later; still, he felt no malice from the apparently dangerous animal.

It had just killed the largest mountain lion Rusty had ever seen in the blink of an eye, and it had all appeared so effortless. He'd never seen anything like it. Despite the impression the cat had on Rusty, he now saw that it never had a chance. He wondered how many wolves the dog had killed in the past. That was when he could have sworn the animal smiled. Maybe it was only in its eyes, but Rusty smiled back despite his wounds. Dog wouldn't have him for dinner. The canine wasn't just another shadow. It was his friend.

Rusty looked at the dog and huffed in a weak voice, "Becoming old was the dumbest thing I've ever done. I thank ya kindly just the same." He tried to smile.

The mountain man lay on the ground where the cat attacked him. Levi held his hand to his face to keep the flapping skin in place. Two broken ribs protruded from his torn buckskin shirt. His grizzly skin coat lay slashed on the ground, but it was all he had. He wrapped it around his body and tried to stand, but the pain was too severe. He lay back in the snow as the white powder turned a dark red. Blood pooled in icy puddles beneath Steel's body.

He stared at the sky, wondering what would happen next. Things still spun around and around but slower, almost lazily. He couldn't remember what time it was or what he was doing lying on the ground staring into space. Rusty felt a cold chill rack his body. White clouds like cotton balls passed between him and the heavens.

He blinked as his peripheral vision started to shrink. Everything around it became hazy and then dark. His sight became smaller and smaller until they were no more than pinpoints staring at a light blue sky. Then the light snapped shut, and there was only darkness. The pain disappeared, as did all thought when he fell into unconsciousness.

The dog looked up from its meal and sniffed the air. It narrowed its eyes at the man lying on the ground. It buried its nose in the snow, wiping away most of the blood, and licked its lips. It walked over to the still body with its mouth open and tongue hanging out. It sniffed Rusty and nudged his shoulder with its snout, but he didn't move. It sniffed his face and then licked the blood away like it did with its own wounds. Its saliva had natural antiseptics to help heal the cuts, slashes, and torn skin.

Never did it growl or do anything but lick. It instinctively cared for the human who had fought for him when facing the four ravenous wolves. Dog's belly was full, so it curled up in the snow next to the wounded man and fell into a calm sleep.

The sun cared little if the man lived or died. Despite all the chaos in the world, it rose and set in the sky just like the day before and the day before that. In the wilderness, the sun and the moon were the only constants one could count on—that, along with danger and violence, which seemed to lurk at every turn. The only safe place to stay these days was back at the compound. Now all that was too late. Hindsight was a hard thing to swallow. If only jealousy hadn't stung Rusty Steel.

MISSING

FOUR STREAMS OF SMOKE SNAKED INTO THE CLEAR BLUE sky from the three cabins and one tipi in the compound. The air was crisp, and it was cold. Scattered snowflakes floated slowly to the ground. The wind had died down, and the trees had stopped swaying. It was cold, but the sun was out to warm a man's face. There was a new addition to the small group of dwellings lost in the wilderness. It wasn't another White man's cabin but was a Crow Indian tipi. For a change at the end of the day, the mountain men filed into the new buffalo skin lodge. It was large and accommodating, even for nine people.

Of course, a war chief had a more sizable and nicer home than most of the tribe, like the chief's, whose was even more extensive. It was part of the honor of holding the position. The door flap facing east was open, allowing fresh cold air to mix with the warmth inside. The interior of the tipi was as warm as toast and smelled of burning wood. The sun hung over the ragged horizon suspended in midair like it was reeled into the sky.

When Rusty didn't return, nobody thought anything about it. They were all busy helping the new couple build their home. Eight of the people living in the compound busied themselves with the chores. They were all amazed when the new home was built in only a few days. Now they were all inside as the fire danced in their eyes. Each one felt an accomplishment and was happy to see Levi so content. A wife was the last thing he was looking for, but it happened so fast that he hardly noticed it from one moment to the next. They were both overwhelmed with feelings.

Like a small army of ants, they toiled from first light until dusk. They cleared the ground of snow, stones, and stumps and laid the floor. Next went up the long slender poles that circled the cone. Finally, the buffalo hides and elk furs were sewn together to make their dwelling weather-tight. They added a smoke flap at the vent and a roll-up buffalo skin door to keep the cold out and the heat in. Several men could stand inside without brushing their shoulders.

At first, Levi was startled and even surprised that his new girl wanted to make up a tipi this time of year. But he, like the other mountain men was completely surprised at how nice it was and how quickly it was assembled.

"Now, if we have to move, it will take us a day to take the tipi down and another day to build it again in some other place," Dahteste said. "This is how the nomadic Plains Indians live."

"And it's as warm as a bread oven." Levi smiled.

Of course, they weren't formally married yet. That would come when they returned to the Dahteste Crow tribe, where the chief could wed them if he would do the honor. They assumed he gave them his blessing when he didn't protest when she left with Levi Johnson after the confrontation with the Blackfeet warriors. The Crow camp was a little higher in the mountains, only a few hours' ride, but she believed the time had to be right too. She wanted to leave sometime between the death of her war party and when they visited. It was best to let the families grieve and not be reminded of what happened with her presence.

Rusty had taken off nearly as soon as they arrived back from facing down the Ute and Blackfeet Indians. Angus felt he was put off because Levi was proving to be more of a mountain man than even, he, despite the fact Steel had to round up the massive Crow war party to save Will, Levi, and Dahteste. She was an essential member of Hachta's tribe, so the chief was eager to help. He appeared to have a soft spot in his heart for the war chief. He treated her with respect. It was rare for a woman to be honored like she was.

What was really bothering Rusty Steel was he felt he had suddenly aged. Like he and Angus had said, if they were young, they would have gone with them or struck out on their own to search for new springs and ponds to trap beaver. Now he saw himself when he was young in Levi Johnson, and he also saw the difference in him now. He had never really pondered on his age, but now that he did—he suddenly felt he was running out of time, so he struck out with his trusty mule and went hunting. He didn't even have a clear direction to go in. He knew the higher he went in the mountains, the worse he could expect the weather to be.

Steel struggled with the aging process. Sure, he could still hold his own in pretty much any situation that arose in the wilderness, but he knew the time for his decline was just over the horizon with the sun. It was slipping away much faster than he expected. Soon it would dawn on him, and he would have to step aside for the younger men just like Angus McFarlin did just recently, although he still did most of his old chores. Dennis Breed was getting on in years, too, and Yosemite Bob was even older. He seemed shorter every year, and his gray hair was whiter. Even his handlebar mustache was white on the waxed tips.

"I wouldn't worry too much, pilgrim," Dennis Breed said. "He's been wanderin' off every so often ever since he came to live with us. I reckon he probably did the same when he lived with the Indians before us. I don't know how such a fiddle-footed man could live on a ship all his life when he seems never to get enough of travelin' through the wilderness." His gold tooth flashed in the firelight when he smiled, and his eyes danced with mischief.

"I agree," Angus said, "but he ain't been himself of late. He seems moody about gettin' old. I told 'im to do like me and just deal with it and carry on like it ain't creepin' up on us. There ain't nothin' we can do about anyway, so ya might just as well ignore it comin'. At this point, there ain't no sense in worryin' about tomorrow when we might not even be here. Only an old fool would worry about what might not be. You can only dodge bullets for so long. While you youngins were gone, he talked about how we used to do the same. Now we don't wander off so often of a winter. I figure he's just reminiscin' a spell. I wouldn't take offense, Levi— William. You know how he feels about y'all. He wasn't in a huff over havin' to come and get cha. He wouldn't have it any other way. He made us all go too, even old Bob."

"Oh, I ain't offended none," Levi replied. "It's just of late things seem to come at us one after another. I thought it was gonna be a quiet winter trappin' a few streams and workin' skins, but up till now, we've hardly had time to breathe. We're lucky we're all here and still alive."

"Welcome to the life of a mountain man. At least we've got plenty of pelts." Yosemite Bob grinned as he twisted the tips of his droopy mustache. "I worry about my next meal more than my age. We're all dyin' a little bit at a time anyway. Right, from the moment we're born, we begin walkin' toward our graves. For some folks, it ain't such a long walk, and for others like us, it lasts a bit longer. I believe the secret is livin' up here where it's healthy."

"Healthy if you don't lose your scalp," Forrester snorted.

"Worryin' about somethin' never changed a dad-gummed thing," Portland Pete said. Beads of sweat sprouted on his face making the pockmarks seem more profound in the light of the tipi. "If you stay here long enough, your mind stops wandering all over the place, and most of your worthless thoughts and noise go silent. That's when you know you've found peace, and it don't matter how old or young you are. If you can still appreciate beauty, that's enough. It's all about enjoyin' what ya got, be it a little or a lot."

"We can always go out and track him down," Forrester said. "We can organize ourselves and spread out like spokes in a wagon wheel until we find signs of fresh tracks. It snowed again last night, so there probably won't be much sign of tracks anymore, but there may be something. I think we can have a scouting patrol ready within the hour."

"I don't think we need to send out a patrol, *Captain*." Levi smiled, but Will didn't get the irony. He was already planning a military type of rescue party, and they didn't even have any sign that he was even in trouble yet.

"How about we wait until we get some sign of a problem before we all go runnin' off like a bunch of scalded chickens." Syracuse Sam laughed, pulling off his raccoon cap as he scratched the scar on the top of his head from where he was scalped. "Y'all got mister paranoia sittin' on your shoulders. Back in the day, old Rusty would take on two or three braves at once and win hands down and all just for the fun of it. I reckon it don't feel too good when that ain't any longer possible. I doubt he's lost much of his touch, though. Livin' up here, we get plenty of practice, don't we now."

"Bring that pot of coffee over here, will ya, Captain," Angus said and snickered because he knew it bothered him being reminded. He tipped a jug on the table and spilled a splash of whiskey into his tin cup, then filled it with coffee. He spooned three heaps of sugar into the viscous black liquid and stirred it as he watched it swirl. "Before anybody else mossies on out into the wilderness this winter, let's make sure Rusty's in trouble. It might take us a day or even two to find a sign of what direction he went in if we can find any sign at all. I asked him where he was going, and he said he didn't know, and it didn't matter. It struck me strange at the time, but sometimes Rusty is a strange fella. If we do find 'im and there's nothing wrong, there will be hell to pay for disruptin' his peace and quiet."

"I'm willing to risk tickin' 'im off if it's for his own good," Levi said. "I've got a bad feelin'.

"Me too," Forrester added. "Like I was saying..."

"If a man pays attention to every bad feeling he got living in the wilderness, he'd never eat," Dennis interrupted and chuckled. "The only ones of us worried about Rusty are you two young fellas."

"I know 'im wiser than any of y'all, so I'll be makin' the decisions of if and when we decide he might be in trouble," Angus said. "I've lived off and on with the Crow just like Rusty. It used to be if he disappeared for a month or two, we never gave it a second thought. I reckon now that he's pushin' fifty, he figures he'll have to test himself to see if he's still got what it takes. Oh, sure, he can still shoot the wings off a fly, but can he weather the worst Mother Nature's got to throw at 'im? That's the more important question here."

"I guess you're right," Levi said, "but I still don't feel comfortable after all that mess with the Ute and Blackfeet hostiles. What happens iffin he runs into another war party?"

"He was dodging bullets long before you were born, son," Angus said. "I reckon he's still young enough to dodge a few more. You boys, just keep your eyes on the sky during the day. If you're worried and he ain't sent up no smoke signals, you're worryin' because y'all wanna. I personally got other things to think about. We've still got a passel of skins to cure, now we've got you tipi built. I figure we best get to work on what we plan to sell next summer."

"What are your friends saying?" Dahteste asked. "I understand a few words, and then I get lost in the conversation."

"That's why I want ya to learn to speak English," Levi replied in Crow. "Oh, sure, they all know a bit of Crow, but not enough to hold a conversation. Everybody exceptin' Angus and Rusty, of course. Angus learned from his wives—he's had a few. And Steel when he lived with the tribe."

"You would think they would learn the language of the people they lived near," Dahteste replied. "If for nothing else, out of respect for the Crow."

"That's one of the things you'll find with folks who speak English." Levi chuckled. "They hate to learn other languages and believe everybody ought to learn theirs. If I'm not mistaken, this whole danged country will speak English one day."

RUSTY STEEL

THE ANCIENT DOG'S EYES POPPED OPEN, AND ITS EARS twitched as it sniffed the air. It scratched the back of its ear with its hind leg, then got up and nudged the human's shoulder again, but still nothing. Then it licked his face, but he didn't move, yet the dog knew the man was still alive. He could hear his heartbeat and shallow breathing with his powerful canine ears. He sniffed the air and smelled the flesh. It noted the first signs of rot. The dog began to clean the wounds on the unconscious man's body. Of course, a dog, no matter where they came from, couldn't reason like a human, but its feeling of contact with the man had stuck, and it patiently waited for him to wake again.

When the wolves were attacking, the dog instinctively understood the man was trying to protect him. He had been successful too, and the dog won the prize. Of course, that first contact was why the canine, in turn, saved the man from the mountain lion, even though the predator had been tracking them both.

During the first night, another pack of wolves

neared where the man lay—or maybe the same wolfs came back to try again. They smelled the blood like the coyotes, but only the larger canines were a threat. Dog spent the whole night beside its new master, growling, snarling, and snapping to keep the hungry predators away. When daylight came, and the scavengers vanished until the sun disappeared again, the dog lay beside the man again, curled up in a ball, and fell into a deep sleep. It hadn't gotten a wink the night before.

When Rusty began to come around, the first thing he noticed was the excruciating pain. He still was too foggy to remember what had happened. His eyeballs fluttered under his eyelids. Fighting against the fog, he tried to clear his head from the screaming hammering between his temples.

Eat the pain! his mind screamed. 'Take it like a man! You must remember what happened!'

His body was so stiff it felt like old wood. It was fragile and brittle from the beating. Still, he couldn't remember who it was who beat him. For a lingering moment, he remembered the Ute and Blackfeet war party, but that was days ago. That was when he noticed the cold. He forced his blood-caked eyes open, but the light was so bright he had to close them again immediately, and he started to shiver. He knew he was covered in the grizzly skin coat, so he probably had a fever. Sweat glistened in the sun on his face and forehead.

His head pounded with each beat of his heart. There was an excruciating pain coming from his chest. He raised his arm. It wasn't broken, nor was the other. He tried to wiggle his toes in the moccasins, and they, too, moved. At least he didn't appear to be on death's door or, even worse—paralyzed, but he could feel a fever clutching at his soul.

Still, he was confused and couldn't remember what happened. He listened for his mule but not a sound. She must have run away. It was a shame because she wouldn't last long in the winter. Many of the predators of the Rockies were hungriest in the winter months when food began to get scarcer. Only the most rugged animals survive the cold winters. If caught out even for a few hours alone, it would fall prey to some predator.

He held his hand over his eyes as he squinted and dared to sneak a peek. What they saw nearly gave him pass out again. Large white canine teeth inside a panting mouth with a long red tongue hanging out the side hovered over him, but he didn't feel threatened. He was immediately sure the dog was protecting him. He didn't know why, but he felt it in his gut. That was when it all came back to him like the rushing rapids of a wild river.

Thoughts and memories burst the dam and filled his mind with information. He and the mountain lion had battled it out, and the massive dog standing watch over him attacked and killed the cat. He looked up at the dog, and they locked eyes. Some strange type of intelligence was in them, which startled the aging mountain man. He had never seen a dog look at him like that. Again, he wondered where it had come from. It was covered in scars and matted hair. It looked as wild as the wildest wolves and twice as big. Its canine teeth were the size of a woman's pinky finger.

Most dogs he had seen since he left St. Luis had been Indian camp dogs. They hung around the strongholds to alarm the Indians when strangers neared. Of course, on the ship, their only pets were cats to catch and eat the mice and rats that snuck aboard up the long mooring lines that stretched like fingers to the docks. This dog didn't look anything like that. It was as tall as a man on its hind legs and weighed well over a hundred thirty pounds. It had long black shaggy hair that surrounded its green eyes. They seemed to stare deep into Rusty's. A shiver ran up his spine, and goosebumps sprouted on his arms and legs.

He looked down as he pulled open his coat. It had long slices in the skin where the mountain lion's claws cut it like a surgical knife. He stared at the ribs poking out of his chest. That was the source of the pain. It wasn't his first busted rib, but he wondered how he would fit the two back together. He raised an arm and tapped the end of the broken bone with his finger. Pain throbbed through the shattered ribs.

Rusty pushed himself onto his elbows as he screamed out in pain. He forced himself despite the feeling a knife was plunged into his chest. He tried to push himself into a sitting position, but it was too much. His head began to spin again, and he was so dizzy that his eyes crawled back into his head, and he fell back into the bloody snow under him. The dog blinked and shook its coat from its head to its tail. It sniffed the air like it was checking for more trouble but found none.

The dog walked up to Rusty and opened its jaws and snapped them closed on the collar of his grizzly bear coat. The canine began to drag the unconscious body through the snow. The slippery surface made a difficult task easy. The dog dragged the dead weight to its den nearby. The entrance to the cave was so small a man had to get down on all fours to gain access, but once inside, it opened into a small cavern. Broken bones scattered the ground at the entrance. Some skeletons were small and others large, but none were human, although a couple looked like wolves.

With such a small entrance, little light penetrated the interior. Tiny black eyes blinked from the ceiling as skin-covered wings flapped silently. The sound of rats and mice scurried in the darkness. The dog's green eyes shone in the dimmest of lights. The only other thing visible was the dull shine of its massive white teeth. It panted over the sleeping man's body, then lay down and went back to sleep.

THE NEXT TIME Rusty Steel awoke, he was even more confused. Maybe it was all just a bad nightmare, he thought, but the pain was still there when he went to move. It was a nightmare, but it was as real as the daylight outside. He saw rays of light enter the small entrance. He looked up into the darkness. Again, he tried to sit up, and this time he made it. He leaned his back against the cold stone wall. It sent another shiver up his spine, but he miraculously didn't feel feverish. He looked down at his broken ribs and knew what awaited him.

He wondered how far the mule wandered before it was killed and eaten. He doubted it made it far with the wolves so close. They probably killed the mule after Dog ran them away. He could try to patch himself up if he could get to his supplies. There, he had whiskey to disinfect the wound. He wondered what happened to his knife. He would need it to seal the wounds closed once he tried to put the bone back together. He would need the whiskey for that too. If not, he would probably pass out again. He had to try to stay conscious. Every time he lost consciousness, he risked losing his life.

Dog lay beside Rusty with its eyes wide open as it watched what the man did. There was no fear between them, only some strange comfort that Rusty felt from the canine and the dog apparently felt from him. The man reached over and patted the dog on the head, and it wagged its tail.

"I reckon I owe you my life a couple of times, there, old boy," Rusty said. He tried to smile, but his mouth wouldn't budge from a hard line. The dog looked back, confused, as it tilted its head and furrowed its eyes. He wondered what the man said.

The mountain man looked around the floor until he found a stick of wood. He peeled the bark off and stuck it between his teeth. He couldn't move without risking puncturing a lung, so he had to set it right then and there. He wished he had the whiskey but couldn't risk looking for it. He still didn't know how far the dog had dragged him. He wondered if he pulled him farther away from the mule or closer. He was going to have to find out.

He looked at the dog as he bit down on the stick and used both hands to pry the first broken bone straight again. Luckily it slipped right back into place, but the pain was so severe Rusty nearly went out again. He had to stop for half an hour to try to do the worst of the two. He struggled to gobble air as his heart raced a hundred miles an hour. It beat so fast he thought it was going to stop. The throbbing in his head was nearly as bad, and he wondered if it would have a stroke. The first one had been easier than he had hoped. He doubted the one sticking out of his chest would be so easy.

He spat out two pieces of the stick—he had bitten it clean in two. He looked around for another fatter piece of wood. He fumbled with it in his trembling hands, dropping it three times before finally getting it to his chattering teeth. He grabbed the bone on the second rib and screamed as he bit the wood, sinking his teeth deep into the grain. He heard a loud snap as the two pieces of rib popped back into place, but now there was a gaping hole in his side where the bone had torn the flesh open.

The blood drained from Rusty's face, and he got dizzy again. He tried to stop it, but the light in his peripheral vision shrank again until the pinpoint went dark, and he returned to somewhere deep in his consciousness where there was no pain or suffering. At least he had gotten the bone set, but now he had to find something to wrap the wound and busted ribs. The whites of his eyes stared blindly at hundreds of bats hiding in the dark.

THE CROW CAMP

EVERYBODY IN THE COMPOUND WAS SURPRISED WHEN THE smoke signals showed up on the edge of the horizon. The black smoke stood out against the snow-covered mountains and the light blue sky. The message confused all the mountain men. Even Dahteste was surprised they were being summoned to the big Crow camp. It wasn't the customary cordial invitation either, but it appeared to be a direct order from Chief Hachta. This made it something they had better consider complying with. You never knew what was happening with the local Indians, especially after so much contact with enemy tribes.

Everyone in the compound was on edge. They had nearly forgotten that Rusty had wandered off to God knows where. Now they didn't even have time to consider going out and looking for him. All their attention was focused on the ominous message sent via puffs of smoke. It was so clear it seemed to scream the message. They all wondered if the chief was still angry about bringing Forrester's uncle, the infamous army

Indian fighter to their camp, or if it was to do with Daht-este and Levi. That, too, could be the source of the problem.

Nobody even asked for the chief's blessing or permission. Johnson simply ran off with one of his war chiefs. Was that the root of the message, and were they all in trouble? Lately, they had seen the first signs that they might not be as welcome on the mountain as they had initially been. A lot had happened that winter, and a lot of it the Crow chief didn't like. Nobody was expecting a welcoming reception. This was just another case of the unknown dangers of living in the wilderness. Even the Crow woman was concerned. This just made the White men more paranoid.

"What in the world is the chief on about now?" Angus asked. "I wish Pine Needle was here or, even better, Rusty Steel. He's the one that's such good friends with the chief."

"But you stay there with your Crow wife more than Rusty does," Forrester said. "You should know him better than anybody. Even old Rusty."

"You know how big that camp is, don't cha," Angus replied. "I hardly go out of Pine Needle's tipi when I'm there in the winter months. That's the time of the year when she dotes on me the most. That's why I always mosey on over to her place about Christmas time and spend the cold months in the stronghold. But that don't mean the chief invites me to dinner. Why, I hardly go out except to do my business. Not with the way Pine Needle cooks." He got a dreamy face just thinking about it. "I might as well pack to stay. It's already late enough in the winter. That is iffin the chief ain't decided to throw us all off his mountain. Then we'll be in a fine mess."

"Well, what are we supposed to do now?" Levi asked as his eyes narrowed. "Rusty's the one who invited us to live up here, and he ain't even here to defend our presence. Technically all of us except Dahteste are trespassin'."

"It would be just like him to disappear on us like that," Angus grumbled. "Every time you need the man, he up and wanders off."

"We can't go without 'im, can we?" Levi asked. "It don't seem right to head out when we don't know if he's all right or not."

"You're the one who has it in your head that something happened to 'im, not me." Angus cackled. "Like I told ya, he'll be fine on his own. Of course, we can go without 'im. Or do you propose to tell the man who lets us live on his land that we don't feel like comin' when he says? I doubt he'd look kindly on us ignoring a direct invite like this one. Iffin, we don't go; we might offend his honor, and that would cause a stink that would put a pole cat to shame."

Dahteste tugged on Levi's buckskin sleeve and said in Crow, "Come on, we have to get ready to go. I don't want to leave Chief Hachta waiting. He is still my leader, and I answer to him. That's the way of our people, and theirs is nothing I can do."

"Whatcha, think he wants with us, darlin'?" Levi asked. "I'm getting that bad feelin' in my gut again."

"You've almost always got a bad feelin' in your stomach," Bob snickered. He was too old to worry anymore. "Stop you frettin', and let's get a move on so we don't make the head honcho wait for us. He'll be countin' the time it takes us to respond. Chiefs don't take well to waitin' on anybody that ain't a chief too. Even war chiefs have to toe the line, don't they, girl."

Dahteste stared at the old man with the walrus mustache with a puzzled face. She still didn't understand much of what the White men said in English. Lucky for her, Levi was a quick student and already had a good start with what Rusty Steel had taught him in as far as Crow. Then she looked at all the White men. They were looking to her for an answer.

The look she gave him spoke a thousand words, and they all saw it. Not going was not an option that the chief would consider acceptable. That much was as clear as water just by the look on her face and the fire in her eyes. Angus flinched when she stared at him. Nobody doubted she was a Crow war chief, even if she was Levi's woman.

"That bad, huh?" Levi replied. "I reckon there ain't anything else to do then. Forrester, make Rusty a note tellin' 'im the chief has called up to the camp. We don't want him to come home, think something has happened, and come lookin' for us. I wonder what in the world is goin' on now."

"I don't know if I like this or not." Forrester frowned, his brow furrowing. "Every time I've been in that camp, I get the feeling I'm never going to leave. Maybe it's just the soldier that's still left in me."

"I've got a feelin' that we don't have anything to say in the matter," Levi huffed. "If Dahteste says we go—we go, or we may just get ourselves kicked off the mountain even before Rusty gets back, if not worse."

"If you want, I can stay," Will Forrester said.

Dahteste turned and said, "The captain goes too," in

English. She was learning fast. "If you no go, it very bad for you. Especially the bluecoat."

"Bluecoat?" Forrester asked.

"Where'd ya learn a word like that?" Levi asked his girl.

"All Indians know the English word for bluecoat," Dahteste said.

"I believe that makes sense." Forrester smiled. "Don't worry, ma'am, no offense taken."

Dahteste looked at the captain, puzzled, then turned her eyes to their tipi and tugged on Levi's sleeve again. "Come, come. No time."

"Go get the horses saddled up," Angus said. "I reckon we can risk it this one time. The arthritis in my feet don't take kindly to the cold snow anymore. That comes from all those years wadin' in the freezing streams."

Levi looked at his friend as his wife continued to pull on his shirt.

"Don't worry, partner," Forrester said, smiling. "I'll take care of the horses, and you take care of Dahteste. I wouldn't dare cross her if I were you."

Forrester opened the door, and the freezing cold hit him in the face like an open slap. At first, his breath clouded his vision. He followed the ice cycle-draped rope to the stables and corral. All the horses were inside, where it was warm as they slept. Nearly an hour later, the captain trailed eight horses to Angus's porch, where everybody was waiting with their bedrolls and saddlebags. With their fur coats and caps, they looked like a half dozen bears waiting on a ride.

The horses groaned as they stepped astride with their supplies behind their saddles. They wheeled them toward the north entrance to the compound. Smokeless chimneys stood above the cabins, and heavy timber shutters covered all the windows. Nobody expected people to come up this far this time of year, but there were still wild animals out there. Until the end of November, even the odd grizzly bear could still be looking for its last meal before heading for its den to sleep for the winter.

The horses blew and nickered as hooves crushed the icy surface of the snow. Even on the trail, which is usually swept with the wind, the horses stood to their knees in the white powder.

"Lucky for the animals, it ain't too far to the Crow camp," Angus said. He was so buried in bear fur you could hardly see his face. The only sign a man was inside was his breath in the cold air.

The half-day it usually took to get to the Crow camp proved to take longer with the snowy conditions. Big white flakes still fell on their hats and caps like autumn leaves. Small drifts of white powder covered the tops and brims. Despite the cold, climbing higher into the mountains made the horses' necks glisten with sweat.

Angus had planned ahead and had his saddlebags full of tobacco and coffee, and he even had one of his old pistols to gift the Crow chief. Still, the old mountain man wondered why he had called them to the camp on such short notice and in nearing the dead of winter. He couldn't help but believe it was trouble.

Of course, they had joined forces against their common enemies, the Blackfeet, and the Ute Indians. But enemy tribes had done the same in the past to fight against another common enemy, the White men, and the United States Army. He wondered what was in store for them now. Maybe Rusty Steel was lucky to be away when the message came.

Despite Angus being married to a Crow woman from the same camp, he still couldn't figure out what Hachta wanted with him. If he contacted them at all, it was always via Rusty Steel. He and Angus were the only ones that red smoke signals, as good as the very Indians who made them. At least they could read the Crow signs. Other tribes used different signals so they could trick their enemies.

Angus rode point in case the hidden Crow guards saw White men coming up the mountain. They should already know they were coming, but it was best to be as careful as possible in such situations. McFarlin knew that if the Indians were angry, there was always the chance a loose warrior would strike out on his own and attack them anyway. In the Indian world, it was easier to ask for forgiveness than for permission. Everybody knew the chief of the tribe couldn't totally control his warrior, and once in a while, they went off on their own and stuck one of their enemies.

Captain Forrester rode drag. His constant state of paranoia had him looking at every shadow, believing they were the enemy. He swung back around every hour and waited to ensure nobody was tailing them. After the last incident, when he and Levi got captured, he wasn't taking any chances, but he found nothing out of order and didn't even see the Crow guard hidden in the shadows and challenging places to see.

Levi and Dahteste rode stirrup to stirrup. She sat in her saddle with her head high. It was apparent she was a fine horsewoman. Just how she sat atop the mare showed how graceful she was as she moved in rhythm with the animal's movements. Her black hair spilled over her shoulders and down her back and shone in the sunlight. She had her bow and a quiver of arrows strapped across her back. Her brand-new pistol stuck out of her belt. Levi had given it to her upon their return.

It was more for her than an enemy. Most mountain men believed if they could, they would end their lives themselves before facing torture. Of course, that all depended on if they caught you by surprise or not. The last time, they luckily didn't have time to shoot themselves. It was a good thing, too, because Rusty had rescued them and saved the day. Still, since the Comanche attacks in Kansas, the fear of capture had stayed in the back of their minds. Especially after they were both captured so quickly, all it took was a combination of wrong events, and you could find yourself on the wrong end of a dozen arrows.

The look on Dahteste's face gave all the men pause. She hadn't planned on returning to her home until the spring. Then when she arrived, she wouldn't be the center of conversation due to the loss of her warriors and the massive turnout of braves to save her and the White men. But now it was too late for that. Her face was steely, and her big brown eyes were as hard as flint. Her expression didn't give anything away except how serious the summons was. She had never heard of such a thing, but this was her first time with White men. She looked over at Levi with concern, but his face, too, was hard to read.

Everybody rode up the mountain on the single trail to the Crow camp from their compound. An uncomfortable silence fell over the travelers. Each and every one wondered what was in store for them at the end of the trial. This trail was made by Mountain Dennis more than a decade before. Back then, it wasn't as well-traveled as now. Over the years, the Crow Indians and the mountain men had seen more and more of each other. Maybe now they were seeing too much of the White men.

One White man brought two, and two White men brought a half dozen. They seemed to be like magnets, and the compound was slowly growing. Something all the men that lived there suddenly became very aware of. First, it was Levi Johnson and Captain Forrester in the summer, and now in the winter, a Crow war chief no less. The mountain men only saw the message being trouble for them all. They all felt the compound was getting too big. Nine people now lived in the group of homes. That was more than ever agreed on.

MAN & DOG

IN RUSTY'S DREAM, HE WAS BACK IN THE CROW CAMP before he left and came to live with Dennis and Angus in the compound in the Rocky Mountains. He lived on the Great Plains and even had his woman. This was something he had never shared with his newfound friends. He wanted it to be a special memory for him alone. He dreamed his Crow bride was kissing his face. He beamed, his face glowing with happiness. It was the last time he had been with a woman. He thought it wouldn't bother him when he left, but he was wrong. He had regretted it ever since.

Despite his friendships, he still had a hole in his heart that he knew now was too late to fill. Seeing Levi and Dahteste had brought back the memory like a kick in the stomach—it took his breath away. Confusion filled his mind as he traveled through time and space. He pinched himself to make sure it wasn't a dream. What did all this mean? Clear objects turned fuzzy and became hard to discern.

He narrowed his eyes and tried to see past his

woman. Who was there waiting? Some objects became all smoky and vanished in the breeze. He looked down, and he could see through his arm. It was like his being was drifting away like smoke from a chimney.

Again, his fiddle-footed nature took him yet to another lifetime. He felt her hot breath on his face. His eyes darted around under his closed eyelids. Somehow, he knew it was just a dream but engaged in it just the same. Her memory made him feel all tingly inside again. He tried to open his eyes to gaze at her beautiful face, but he could feel her but not see her no matter how hard he tried. He felt every feature of her curvy body, but the face framed by her shining black hair evaded his gaze.

Then Rusty suddenly remembered she was dead, and he must be talking to her ghost. It suddenly occurred to him that maybe he was a ghost too. A shudder ran through the pain-racked body, bringing him to the edge of his dream. He was on the threshold of stepping into the real world again. His breathing quickened and became shallow. Beads of sweat stood on his brow and upper lip. His body quivered as if there was an earthquake, but nothing moved. Suddenly the ground under him vanished, and he began to fall. He felt his body spinning around and around.

When Rusty woke up, he could hear the dog panting over him with its warm breath on his face. It was licking the crusty blood from his broken skin. For a second, the mountain man froze. If it got the taste of his blood, would it get hungry and eat him? In his condition, he couldn't do much to stop it. He wondered if the powder in his guns was still dry, but he doubted it. He couldn't remember how long he had been in the cave. Despite his being accustomed to the cold, his body temperature plummeted without a fire. He knew what he had to do next to survive.

His ribs shot bolts of pain through his body every time he attempted to move, but he knew he would have to fight the pain and get some wood to warm him before he lost his toes and fingers—maybe even his ears and nose. He had seen firsthand what frostbite did to the small digits and extremities. He looked at his fingers, which were just turning dark on the tips. He knew time was of the essence. He felt in his buckskin shirt pocket. It was full of everyday necessities for a mountain man. Among those possessions were a flint and striker.

He wondered where his knife was. It had to be back where the mountain lion attacked him, wherever that was. Only the dog knew right now. He felt around inside his frontiersman's pocket, pulled out some hardtack, and chewed on it with a desert-dry mouth. He needed water desperately too. He crawled to the entrance, scraped snow into his hands, and gobbled it up as it slowly quenched his thirst.

He peered out the small entrance to the cave—he used his hand to shade the glare. Luckily the recent snowfall had been light, and he could still see the bloody trail where the dog dragged him through the snow. At least it would be easy to follow. He wondered if he could get to his feet yet. Since he set the ribs, the pain hadn't subsided, but he felt more mobile. He pushed himself to his knees, then caught his breath as bolts of pain shot through his body.

"As long as I feel pain, I'm still alive," Rusty whispered.

The dog turned and looked at the human curiously

as it tilted its head—it seemed almost to have human intelligence. It sat patiently to see what he was going to do. He put a foot to the ground and boosted himself up. His head spun, and he dropped to one knee again. Rusty wondered if there was damage inside too. He was spitting up blood, but it wasn't too much, which was a good sign. Still, he felt like a bull whacker's cargo wagon had run over him at full speed.

He crawled on all fours through the entrance and into the sparkling daylight. It was so bright it blinded him at first. He had to cover his eyes and accustom himself to the sun flashing off the snow. He pushed himself to his feet again, and this time he was successful. He wobbled a bit but found his center and took his first step.

He felt that once he got his ribs wrapped as tightly as he could, got some hot food in his body, and thawed out by a hot fire, he would feel well enough to work out some plan. At the moment, the only plan was survival, and he knew he wouldn't if he let the cold get to him. He scooped up more snow and slowly quenched his thirst. He found a stick beside the blood trail and used it to help keep his balance. The wind howled through the trees as they swayed. Snowflakes as big as butterflies began to fall. At first, just a few scattered flakes, but soon it began to snow in earnest.

His nose was so cold he couldn't smell anymore, and his hands and feet were numb. Lucky for Steel, he saw the mule after walking for less than half an hour. There wasn't much left of his old faithful friend. The important thing was the supplies seemed to be intact. With a warm, fat mule to eat, the wolves weren't interested in dried beans. The first thing he did was use the bandages he always carried to wrap his ribs. It hurt when he pulled it as tight as he dared, but he could move with less pain once it was tied off. He continued to search for the gun he had dropped and his knife.

After another ten-minute walk, he saw a flash of sunlight in the bright snow. It was the blade of his knife. Beside it lay a dead mountain lion and, besides that, a pistol. It was the biggest cat he had ever seen. He wondered how he survived. He struggled to kneel and recover his knife. He crawled to the dead cat on his hands and knees. He poked it with the knife, but it was as hard as a brick.

What the scavengers hadn't eaten was frozen stiff, and he would need an axe to chop it up unless he could thaw it out and recover the fur. He felt it only fitting he kept the skin of the lion that nearly killed him. He looked back and saw the curious eyes of the dog. No doubt it, too, feasted on the mule and the cat.

On Rusty's way back to the cave, he gathered dead wood he found pushing his feet through the snow. He brought all he could carry and made the short trek back to the small cave. A lightning-racked tree stood by the entrance. When he got everything he needed for the fire, he had to shave some kindling from the dead wood, but he struggled to steady the knife in his freezing hands. Eventually, he used the tiny ball of starter he had in his supplies and lit the kindling; then, the dry wood began to crackle and pop, and smoke filled the cave. But the warmth was worth it.

The small room was suddenly lit with dancing flames. The bats spooked, and some poured out the entrance into the daylight while others silently flapped their hairy wings and took a moment to settle again.

The fire danced in Rusty's eyes as heat radiated from the orange coals. He was so close he could smell the hair on his skin singe, but his body quickly responded. He pulled his snow-drenched moccasins off and dried them before the fire as he wiggled his stiff toes near the flames. He had to be careful not to burn his feet because they were still numb.

Soon the smell of baked beans and pieces of dried beef floated in the air, along with the smell of burning wood. In the wilderness, both were signs of life and survival. Rusty grinned despite the pain and what he still had in front of him. There was a knowing feeling inside him. He knew he still had the skills to survive in the wilderness despite all its dangers.

He pulled his spoon from his frontiersman's pocket in his buckskin shirt and scooped up some beans. Steam streamed from the hot spoon, and he burned his lips, but the hot food settled, glowing in his stomach. Soon he was shoveling food into his mouth as fast as he could. He wasn't even hungry until he had his first bite. Now he realized he was famished.

He looked over at the dog, scooped black beans into a pan, and offered them to his new friend. Its eyes lit up, and it wagged its tail, but still, it was careful, suspecting maybe it was a trap. But it felt no ill will from the human it saved, and it dropped its head and slurped up the meat and beans in seconds. It looked at Rusty, licked its lips, and belched. The aging mountain man laughed until he got a stitch. It was good to feel alive, and a man never felt so alive as just after he nearly lost his life.

When his foot gear was dry, he pulled them back on, opened his coat, and looked at his bandage. Moving around had made the open wound start to bleed again, and the white bandages were stained red. Still, he knew it wasn't a life-threatening injury now that he had a fire. Next, he was going to have to hunt for some food. He would never be able to drag the cat back here by himself. Now it was a stiff dead weight.

He could use the meat now and felt he had earned the fur, but men didn't decide how things worked out in the wilderness. Mother Nature was who decided who died and who survived. He appeared to be one of the lucky ones for the moment, but he still had to heal enough to endure the trek back home. Hopefully, the weather didn't go south on him before then. He looked at the sky, and it had that winter look to it. He figured any day, he would be looking at a blizzard. He would have to decide if the shelter in the cave was preferable to risking the trek back to the compound and his warm and cozy cabin.

He had to chuckle to himself. He had become accustomed to the comforts of having a roof over his head and a warm place to spend the winter. He realized it was high time he returned to his old ways and took on the wilderness face-on. Rusty's eyes glowed orange in the glowing coals. Hot cinders threatened to burn the fur on the hairy animals hanging from the ceiling. He laughed at himself for allowing himself to get soft. He was glad he had struck out as soon as they arrived back at the compound. It was the only way to come to terms with himself and his age.

Sure, part of his feeling was jealousy. He rarely tolerated it, but it was inherent in all normal humans. It was the skill of controlling it was what he admired. He had total control over his feelings and his environment. He still had it in him to take on Mother Nature. He wondered what else she had planned to throw at him before he returned home. That was when it struck him. Maybe he didn't want to go back. At least not quite yet. He still had a thing or two to prove to himself, so he might have to stick it out a few more weeks if not a few months. If he got stuck here for the winter, then so be it. He was prepared to take on any hardships that the Rocky Mountains had to throw at him.

He sat by the fire and pulled out his ceramic pipe. It still hurt to move, but his body was warm, and he had loosened up some. He fished around in his pocket for a twist of tobacco, tearing off a bit to stuff his pipe. He took a burning stick from the fire and puffed it to life. The glowing bowl reflected in his eyes as smoke billowed around his head. After a few puffs, his head nodded to his chest, and he fell asleep snoring softly.

INDIAN DRUMS

THEY COULD ALL HEAR THE DRUMS IN THE DISTANCE EVEN before they saw the smoke snaking out of the vents of over a hundred tipis and almost as many cooking fires. The sound was ominous and seemed to reverberate off the canyon walls and mountain peaks, making them echo over and over as the sound traveled in the crisp air. They all looked at Dahteste, but her face was chiseled in stone. She was so surprised that Chief Hachta summoned them so quickly after their arrival that she wasn't sure what she was hearing.

The beat of the drums just confused her more, but she was ready to face the music no matter where it led her. A worried expression crossed her face, but she just as quickly pushed it away. She allowed her eyes to glance to her side to see if anyone noticed. She never showed her true feeling in such times of tension, no matter what she faced.

Never show your weaknesses, she thought to herself.

That's what she learned as a warrior and taught

others as a war chief. She knew how crafty the chief was and wondered why the drums beat the message they sent. Her world had changed so much in the last weeks that she wasn't sure if she was welcome or not anymore. She wasn't accustomed to this feeling of confusion. Maybe the chief just saved her for punishment later. Everything that had happened in the last weeks had been a contradiction and full of chaos. She had nearly lost her life only to survive and fall into the hands of scalpers. She saw in the leader's eyes what he had planned for her. She would have been forced to be his wife or, better said, his slave.

That is until Levi Johnson came to her rescue. And, of course, Rusty Steel and Chief Hachta with three hundred warriors. The show of force scared all their enemies away, and their lives were spared. But for what? Maybe to be tortured in the end anyway.

She listened carefully, but what the drums beat was a pow-wow and not a war dance. She was as confused as she had ever been in her life, but she wasn't going to show her feelings even to the man she loved. No matter whom she took as her husband, she was still a Crow war chief until Hachta saw otherwise.

You never knew exactly what went on in the mind of the Chief. It was always best to tread carefully. He played each of the tribe's members like a harp, picking different strings to make different effects. Hachta had easily outsmarted every enemy and sometimes played mind games to control his warriors. His cleverness was why he was still their leader; some younger men hadn't taken his position. He was constantly planning three or four steps ahead of the rest and was a master at war games and getting what he wanted from the medicine men and elders.

He had full support from his tribe, so whatever he decided would be written in stone. If she were to be banished, she would go without a word. If punished physically, she would accept her fate like a warrior. She knew she had let the chief and her warriors down.

She couldn't help but blame herself for not expecting an ambush. Honestly, she had always been vigilant, but the scalpers were good at sneaking up on Indians. Her hair had nearly joined all the scalps they had taken that winter from Indian men, women, and even children from all the tribes.

What Dahteste said held little importance in a tribe of so many, even if she was or maybe is still a war chief. That would be for her leader to decide—she felt her fate and future were uncertain. And somehow, she thought she could live in peace with Levi. When a person is in charge of a war party, even if it's small, they were responsible for their deaths, especially if they died without honor.

The drums said the contrary to what she expected— but it could be a trap. The chief knew she would turn and flee if they were war drums. She felt like he was luring her to camp, and maybe he was doing so with false pretenses.

She stepped forward with caution. Maybe there would be braves ready to capture her right before they arrived. She pulled stirrup to stirrup with Levi and clutched his shirt. He dwarfed the Crow woman, and Buck dwarfed her horse too. She didn't have to tell the mountain men to be careful. They were always on their toes when the chief summoned them. It was a very unusual occasion, and in the past, it had rarely been for a friendly visit, especially now that he ordered all the men in the camp to come with Dahteste.

"I figure it can only be one thing," Mountain Dennis whispered. "He's gonna tell us we've gotta leave the mountain. When I first came up here and built the first cabin, I figured they'd run me off in a couple of winters. But they got hooked on coffee and tobacky, and each year, they wanted to trade for more. It's been goin' on like that for decades now. Now I reckon we've become more of a nuisance than an advantage. They can get their supplies from the Rendezvous like everybody else."

"The chief don't like his braves goin' to the Rendezvous because they get drunk and cheated out of their pelts," Levi said. "It's happened every time they go.

"I can't say as I blame 'im iffin he does run us off," Angus huffed. "With all the trouble we've been of late. I figured they'd be after us like scalded chickens after bringing that Indian fighter right into their camp."

"But it was an innocent error of judgment," Will pleaded. "They can't hold it against us for what somebody else did. I'm his nephew, and even I didn't know he was such an evil man. It just wouldn't be fair."

"Be my guest and tell the chief that for us when we get there," Angus huffed. "I sure as heck don't wanna be the first in line. He's got more warriors than bees got honey."

"Fair for who?" Forrester asked. "I guess when you come down to it, we're all responsible for the recent troubles. I hope we didn't get Dahteste into deep too."

"Whatcha think, Dahteste?" Levi asked.

She blinked her big brown eyes but just shrugged. A shrug is a shrug in any language, unlike a shake of the head or nod.

As they neared, the drums became so loud they felt the percussion in their chests as their hearts pounded between their ears. Despite the temperatures, all their faces glistened with sweat. They carefully wheeled their horses up the last hill before opening into the valley. There was a strange absence of Crow warriors and guards. Nobody seemed to be watching, but they knew they were there somewhere, hiding and spying on them like they always did. Forrester could feel the eyes on him, and Dahteste knew from experience that they were there even if they didn't see them.

"This is the strangest welcome I've ever had," Angus said. "I sure wish Rusty was here with us. I doubt the chief be angry with him. He's saved his bacon a time or two. I wonder where Pine Needle is. I wish she was with us. She might know what's goin' on."

"Rusty Steel ain't gonna do us much good with him runnin' off to who knows where," Dennis said as he looked around with his eyes stretched wide.

Levi and Forrester locked eyes for a second. Both were full of questions and no answers. They looked at Dahteste, but she was focused on where her horse stepped and seemed to ignore everybody. Johnson and Forrester believed it was probably intentional. A person couldn't answer questions they didn't have an answer to. She must be just as perplexed as the mountain men.

It was true, though. Now, more than ever, they could use their old friend Rusty Steel. They wouldn't feel nearly as threatened if he was along, but nobody knew where he had run off to, and now his track would be so cold they wouldn't be able to find him even if they tried. Hopefully, he was all right.

The last stretch to the top of the trail was the most treacherous. This was by design rather than chance. The Indians had made the trail to the camp difficult intentionally, so if the mountain men ran off the rails and got aggressive, their access would be held up enough for the tribe to retaliate. Of course, nothing of the sort ever happened, but the Crow knew the mountain men had the potential with their vast array of firearms. They knew this was enough to still consider them a possible threat someday. In the world of the Crow Indians, there were enemies on all sides, just like there had always been.

"It would be the perfect plan to capture us," Captain Forrester said. "They would have us without firing a bullet or arrow. We'll walk right into their arms without a shot fired." His fingers unconsciously tapped on the grip of the pistol in his belt.

"Now you're talkin' nonsense." Levi laughed, but it didn't sound as confident as he would have liked. "They ain't gonna do nothin' to us. Like Dennis says, they'll throw us off the mountain at worst. I can't see the chief allowin' bloodshed, but we have been a nuisance. I reckon Will and me comin' up her to live threw a hammer in the works. We didn't do it intentionally."

"It might not be as far-fetched as you think," Yosemite Bob whispered. "Them drums might be deceivin'. Your woman don't look so sure of herself."

Levi bit his lip. He didn't want to say anything one way or the other. He knew he was in the hot seat if there was a problem with Dahteste, both with the other mountain men and with the chief. Paranoia gripped the party in its clutches as it ate at their stomachs. It was only a few meters to the top, and they would come in sight of the Crow stronghold. Time was running out, and all their minds were banging questions around like a marble in a tin can. They imagined every scenario under the sun, but none were positive. Still, the drums hammered like angry bulls stomping their hooves.

Streams of smoke hung suspended in the sky on a windless day. The trees stopped swaying, and it completely stopped snowing as the sun's rays bounced off the white crystals as far as the eye could see. The only sound was the horses groaning as they climbed the steepest part of the narrow trail. That and the crunching of ice-covered snow. After a while came the occasional nicker or whinny. They were almost there—their animals smelled the Crow horses, and Indian camp dogs began to bark on the outskirts.

Still, the drums hammered, and now they were so loud they drowned out all thought. They climbed to the summit one at a time, stopping before proceeding. The first tipis were just meters away. A massive fire burned before them as flames leaped into the sky. Fiery cinders spiraled up and out of sight. Lazy cotton-like clouds hung suspended in the sky. The wood puffed steam and popped and crackled. Waves of heat radiated from its core and shone on the faces of the Crow Indians circling the fire. In the inner circle sat men before drums with sweat-drenched faces as they slammed their drumsticks into the stretched skins.

Dahteste gasped when she saw the whole tribe assembled. She couldn't imagine why. Chief Hachta sat on a pile of furs on the far side, elevating him above the rest of the Indians. His face, like always, was a mask, impossible to read, and his mouth no more than a gash. Nothing surprised the woman war chief yet. Then she looked into Hachta's eyes, and they locked, and she knew exactly what was happening. Instants after, the rest of the mountain men suddenly understood too.

RECOVERY

WHEN RUSTY OPENED HIS EYES, HE SAW IT WAS DAYLIGHT. He rubbed them with the heels of his hands to clean the sleep away. The cave was always dim, but the sun entering the small entrance during the day made it bright enough to see. He fumbled with the fire, and in minutes he was sitting before a source of heat like the air was a source of life. He wondered if men ever lived without fires, and if they did, who discovered how to make them?

He had seen Plains Indians using several ways to spark an ember in a tinder ball. Of course, all the mountain men use a flint and steel striker. He wiggled his toes near the flames. The blackness at the tips of his toes and fingers had disappeared, so he didn't have frostbite. He was lucky all around. He had survived the attack from the mountain lion thanks to Dog and, until now, had survived the cold. From then on, it all depended on how long it took him to recuperate. He looked across the cave, but his new friend wasn't there. Just like wolves, it was probably out hunting all night.

He knew he couldn't make the trip back to his cabin in the condition he was in. If he lit out now, he wouldn't make it three days. It was an arduous trek for a man in the best of health. He still had to walk and climb, so he had to wait until the wound from the broken ribs healed enough that it wouldn't break open again. At least here, he had a cave to shelter in. The small entrance kept the heat from the fire in too. It was like a large bread oven; when the fire roared, he was as warm as toast. Of course, the first blizzard had yet to hit, so the deep cold hadn't set in. Hopefully, he was back in the compound by then, but he already realized he might have to winter in the cave with Dog.

Steel opened his coat and had a look at the bandage. It wasn't seeping blood anymore. He pulled the cloth aside and saw the wound had a large crusty scab over it, but the skin was still red and puffy all around. If he could stay still enough for it to dry, he believed he would be out of the woods. He thought the cold weather must keep his fever from latching on and killing him, but he still had a stretch to go. He would have to be careful if he wanted to make it home this winter. If he opened the wound again, he would have to wait another week or ten days, and soon it would be too late to chance traveling until March.

He scooped snow from the entrance and melted it in a pan. As soon as it was liquid, he poured some coffee in and let it heat. In minutes, the aroma floated on puffs of air. The bats protested again but finally settled and stopped flapping woolly wings.

After a couple of coffees to wake him up, he crawled to the entrance and was outside, where the sun glared off all the shiny surfaces. Rusty smiled despite his problems. He was deep in the wilderness for the first time in a long time. He suddenly realized that he had achieved his goal and hadn't even realized it. He felt young and full of spunk with a thirst for adventure he hadn't felt for years. This small but dangerous journey had sparked something inside that gave him the boost he needed to take on Mother Nature at her meanest, if that's what it took. Maybe he would spend the winter there anyway. It would give him time to get to know his new friend, Dog, and prove to himself he was as good as ever.

He stood and looked out on the mountains as he relieved himself. Steam rose from the snow. Small gusts of wind pushed white powder across the flat places causing drifts. In the distance, he saw an elk. At first, it didn't notice the human. He watched the beautiful animal and never thought of shooting it. Rusty turned his head to see better, and the animal caught the motion, and they locked eyes. But the mountain man felt no malice toward the animal, only amazement at its beauty. The elk jerked its head and looked away. The black hairy dog came bounding through the snow. When Rusty looked back toward the buck, he just caught sight of its antlers vanishing over the ridge.

"Hey, boy." Rusty smiled. The dog came inbound at a dangerous speed but seemed to sense his human was still delicate and bumped down to a walk. "Where you been, fella?"

The hairy black dog wagged its tail as snowflakes flew through the air. It bounced on its front legs and barked.

"I know ya wanna play, boy, but you're gonna have to wait a spell longer." Rusty chuckled as he scratched its head. "But you just watch. In no time, I'll be as right as rain."

That was when Rusty smelled the wood burning. He instinctively dropped into the snow with only his eyes and cap showing. The dog lay flat too. It sniffed the air and crawled beside its master.

"Whatcha think, boy?" Rusty whispered. "Only men make campfires. We best go fetch my guns and have a look."

Rusty disappeared on all fours into the cave. In minutes he came back out. He had put an extra bandage on his wound and four pistols stuck from his belt. His bow and quiver of arrows were strapped across his back. He knew they needed to find out who was out there before they found out he and his dog were trespassing on somebody's property.

"With the way the wilderness keeps shrinking, maybe this mountain does belong to somebody," Rusty whispered.

He had only assumed nobody lived there. For all he knew, he would be camped near a Blackfoot Indian camp. As he glanced eastward at the sun, he used his hand to shade his eyes. He strapped on his snowshoes and moved across the open space, ducking as low as he could until they reached the tree line and disappeared in the forest's shadows. He hadn't been outside much since the mountain lion attacked him, and the cold slapped him in the face like a skillet. He pushed the discomfort aside, held his side, and carefully moved through the woods, using the shadows to hide his presence.

He followed his nose and Dog as they moved closer to the smell of burning wood. He tried to spy smoke through the trees, but they were too tall and dense. In some places, the snow hadn't even stuck. Still, the odor was strong, especially in the cold, crisp air. Rusty went fifty yards and stopped and listened. Then he would move another fifty yards closer. Each time the smell of burning wood was more pungent. He squatted and listened but still nothing. Then he got up and went for another stretch. But the dog suddenly dropped into the snow, and Rusty followed suit instantly.

That was when he heard men speaking in a language he didn't understand or even recognize. He looked at Dog as it barred its teeth, but it instinctively knew not to growl or make a sound. As they waited, frozen in place, Rusty could hear three different voices. That didn't mean there were only three men because some men didn't have much to say, but it gave him a boost of courage. If they were a challenge, he hoped it was only three. If he caught them by surprise, he could take them. Now he had to be as quiet and careful as possible, or he wouldn't make it. Men out in the mountains this time of year were almost certain Indians. Hopefully, they were Crow, but he doubted it.

Rusty pulled a pistol with each hand and crawled through the snow on his elbows. He was ready to take a bead and fire at the slightest sign of danger. He had four bullets and fifteen arrows, so he knew he had enough firepower for a few braves. Whoever it was out there, he doubted they would be friendly. The White man was everybody's enemy in the deepest forests of the wilderness. Even other White men you might find this time of year could be dangerous. It was a challenging and rugged place, so it was only for rough and rugged men.

The Rocky Mountains seemed to be a magnet for

wayward White men but rarely in the winter months. If only it were White men. There weren't half as dangerous as Indians—especially if they were defending their homeland. No enemy is as ferocious as a man defending his home and family from trespassers. Steam streamed from Rusty's mouth and Dog's nose.

As it breathed, it made little puffs of snow blow away. He heard movement, and the talking abruptly stopped. Footsteps crunched in the snow coming his way, so he buried himself in the deep powder and hoped for the best. He pulled a small limb from a broken pine close to his face so he could spy with one eye. He shoved his mouth into the snow to stop the steam and held his breath.

Three Indians walked by so close to where he lay, he was surprised he wasn't discovered. Rusty couldn't believe they didn't see him. They hadn't even noticed the black fur poking out from the white snow. He carefully followed them to see where they were going. If they were headed to their stronghold, he wanted to know where it was before planning further. Everything could change entirely, just like the weather in the Rockies. A man could lose his life in a breath or two. At least he didn't have to worry about bears. He doubted even Dog would take on a grizzly.

With each step Rusty took, it felt like somebody was stabbing him with a knife. His ribs throbbed with each beat of his heart which drummed between his ears. He could only hope the dog didn't jump up and run off, making noise the warriors might hear. Or maybe even bark, but it seemed to know the game of hunting even better than the mountain man. Again, Rusty Steel wondered what tribe the Indians came from.

Maybe they were friendly, but then again, he hadn't met many amicable Indians other than Hachta over the years. Most of them wanted to run them out of the mountains, and Steel couldn't really blame them. He knew what was quickly happening. It is a wave of people the size of an ocean, so of course, it would affect them all sooner or later, and it looked like it would be sooner.

When the Indians Rusty followed stopped, he saw they had a camp. They had built a provisional shelter from the weather. Piles of frozen cold-water beaver pelts were stacked beside the lean-to. They were trapping, and it looked like they had a bonanza, so they wouldn't be going anywhere until the first heavy storm pushed its way through the mountains. Soon it would be all frozen, making trapping or even moving around difficult. Snow began to fall again. This time the flakes were small but abundant and steady. Rusty backed out the way he crawled in and leaned against a tree. The dog dropped beside him, but the hair on its back was ruffled, and its ears alert. It knew danger was near.

"We best get back to the cave before these boys decide to snoop around," Rusty whispered.

The dog got up and followed with its tail at twelve o'clock. The mountain man still had a pistol in each white-knuckled fist and was on the alert. Now that he knew they weren't alone, he had to look at his position again despite his wound. It wouldn't matter if it healed or not if the Indians found and killed him. Again, he tried to remember where he had seen those types of beads and trim on their moccasins. He knew he had seen it somewhere before but couldn't put a finger on it. Still, he had little to no hope that they were friendly.

Rusty had only met a few friendly Indians in his time in the Rockies; most of them were when he lived with the Crow more than a decade ago. The only reason Chief Hachta was his friend was because he saved his life. It was the only honorable thing he could do. At first, Rusty noticed that although he swore, he owed him, he still didn't trust him. But over the years, one saved the others' bacon on more than a couple of occasions as more White men came to the Rockies. Now they knew each other well and were nearly like brothers. Or as close to brothers as a Crow chief could be with a white mountain man.

When they returned to the cave, he made a fire, lit his pipe, and glared into the cinders. His face glowed orange in the face of the hot coals. He wondered what he should do now. He had very limited options. He supposed the only safe choice was to stay in the cave until he recovered just like he had planned, but now it wouldn't be so safe. He would have to be careful with the fire at night. The mouth of the small cavern faced the valley and was visible on the side of the mountain. If there was a fire inside, the entrance would glow orange against a background of white snow.

CHIEF HACHTA

THE POUNDING OF DAHTESTE'S HEART BEAT SO LOUDLY that Levi was sure he could hear it as they sat stirrup-to-stirrup before the camp. Beads of sweat spread across their brows and upper lips despite their red noses and ears. Buffalo rawhide stretched tight across hollowed-out cedar logs and fastened with sinew thongs, made up the dance circle. The Crow believed the drums were voices making their connection to all creation. It was the sound of a heartbeat and that of all Mother Nature. They believed the rhythm coming from their drums was the foundation of song and prayer and symbolized the link between heaven and earth.

Chief Hachta sat at the head of the circle of six drummers. Medicine men sat to one side and elders at the other. Behind him roared a large fire emitting heat waves three hundred sixty degrees, making the cold winter day bearable. For them, Indian life went on like it did every day despite the weather. Everybody was covered in heavy buffalo and bear skins, and their breaths were visible in the air. A hundred more fires burned across the camp, but most of the tribe's members stood behind the chief. They were all waiting on Dahteste and the mountain men's arrival. The White men they allowed to live on their mountain. The drummers continued to pound on the hides with drumsticks. The sound reverberated in their chests and minds. It was mesmerizing, almost hypnotizing, as the beats mocked that of their hearts.

The party invited to come were all nervous. Nobody gave away a thing but looked at the chief in anticipation. They didn't know why they had been summoned and couldn't help but think the worst. Why else would Hachta order them to attend? It was something that had never happened before, and Dennis had been there for decades.

Johnson's heart stopped cold as he slipped his hand under his buckskin shirt and wrapped his fingers around his pistol's grip—his thumb resting on the hammer. Fear kicked up a notch and got his full attention. Forrester's blue eyes were as hard as steel. He was ready for whatever they were going to throw at them. He knew he was the person most responsible for bringing his uncle to the camp. It could have been the straw that broke the camel's back.

Just one mistake too many for the Crow to accept— that and the sudden increase in population in the compound. They hadn't considered this when at least Rusty should have. It was a delicate balance between being a necessity to being a nuisance to their Indian neighbors. When they arrived at the camp, Chief Hachta looked at them judiciously. He cradled a coffee in his hands, rotating the tin cup, absorbing the heat. Steam rose, disappearing inches from the vessel. Then the chief curled a smile—it was barely noticeable, but it was there. He nodded at the woman war chief.

Dahteste stared at him hard, her eyes expansive. Her face lit up with anticipation. When the truth settled in, her eyes went wide. Her look was filled with joy and vindication.

"Are you ready for your wedding?" Chief Hachta asked. His gaze drifted to Levi Johnson. "You *do* plan to marry my best war chief, don't you?"

First, bewilderment showed on the faces of the mountain men. They didn't know the chief well like Dahteste or Rusty Steel. Each and every one was expecting bad news, and that was a minimum. The captain and Levi were just about to pull their guns, and they would have indeed died, but they would have taken some of them with them. Often unexpected actions were combined with unexpected answers, as in this case. All that pent-up fear and tension suddenly disappeared, and they felt weak and exhausted. Maybe that was part of Hachta's plan too. Only the woman war chief took it in stride. Then again, she rarely showed her feelings. She was harder to read than the chief.

Hachta held up his hand, and the drums instantly stopped. An awkward silence fell over everybody, waiting to hear the following words spoken by their leader, Dahteste, and Levi Johnson. She let out a long breath, relaxing her. She looked at her chief and smiled at him gratefully, the blood rushing back into her face.

All the mountain men took the good news like starving men given inch-thick steaks, and they all breathed relief too. Old Angus stifled a cackle. They knew they were outnumbered thirty to one and wouldn't have had a chance. Lucky for them, they misunderstood the root of the message. It was a pow-wow and not a war dance. Not something that was lost on Dahteste, but she also knew how crafty her chief was. It was true; had the drums been from the war dance, she may have fled to save her life.

Although she was a war chief, she was still only human, and all men and women felt fear. It was the human instinct of fight or flight. Most people chose flight even if they were brave, given the opportunity. All men wished to live another day, and nobody wanted to be shamed by their peers. She was a brave woman but still far from perfect. Not even Hachta was perfect. She had witnessed him commit errors like all men, even though she had to admit it was rare. But she also knew he was always a fair chief. Now she felt ashamed that she believed he would be unfair to her. He never gave her such a reason to think such a thing, but then again, she never lost four warrior braves' lives and nearly her own.

Under the chief's facade, she also knew there was more than one reason he would do such a thing. It was just a matter of time before she discovered what it was. He never made such a significant statement unless he feared losing control of his warrior braves or something as serious. This was indeed a special occasion, but the wedding wouldn't be all that motivated Hachta. She wondered what it was but knew better than to ask. It would all come out in time.

Now it appeared that she and Levi Johnson were

going to get married before they planned. This much she knew. If the chief said they were to wed, they would be married by the end of the day, and nobody was going to contest his decision, even if they weren't quite ready. Then again, who was ready when they suddenly found themselves wed? Her head turned to Levi, and she beamed. He smiled back, although he showed his nervousness. When facing a sure fight, he was ready, but to suddenly be getting married made him more nervous than a dog with ticks.

Chief Hachta motioned for them to dismount and waved his hand for Dahteste and Levi to come and sit before him. Johnson was shocked. Sure, he knew the chief from the visits to the camp with Rusty Steel, and the Crow had helped save them from the Ute, Blackfeet, and the scalpers. But he had never been invited to sit beside him like he had seen Rusty do. It was a special occasion. Levi was being invited into the Crow tribe as an honorary member.

The fact Levi was the best trapper, tracker, and shot of any White man in the Rocky Mountains hadn't gone unnoticed by the chief. He also knew there were several warriors that weren't happy with Dahteste running off with a White man of all things. This was something nobody ever expected, especially her. She was the last Indian in the camp that would have been expected to do such a thing. But the chief knew that love did strange things to most men and women. It wouldn't matter what he said, so he planned to give them his blessing and marry them himself.

Three warriors had been after Dahteste to marry them since they were teens. For them to lose her to someone from outside the tribe was unheard of, and they wouldn't accept their fate easily, but in the end, they would accept it. This was much better than more bloodshed. The chief knew it was the only way to cool the young braves off. They had too much testosterone for their own good. Besides that, the chief actually liked Levi Beaver Johnson. He reminded him of a young Rusty Steel but smarter.

The chief had to make the pow-wow to keep these warriors from going out and doing something stupid. He knew if he ordered a celebration, they would want to attend. They didn't have to know the reason for the pow-wow until he saw fit. Now he planned to get her married to Levi as quickly as possible and cut the blossoming bud of trouble in the nub before it grew and spread. Just like Dahteste had assumed, there was more than one reason for the celebration and even the marriage. She had observed her leader carefully and knew he did everything for a reason, if not a half dozen.

Today they would celebrate, the chief would wed the two, and they would be led to her tipi. Once the marriage was consummated, there was nothing more the belligerent braves could do. He believed Levi Johnson would also be an excellent addition to their tribe. He was already speaking Crow and was young when the chief and Rusty Steel were getting old, and soon their times would be passed. He had secretly always hoped that Dahteste would step up and take his place as chief of the tribe.

There was no reason a woman war chief couldn't become a chief. She had the most level head on her shoulders and knew how to hide her true feelings when needed. He knew exactly what happened when she lost her four warriors. He felt lucky her life had been spared, and he had no intention of losing her just because she decided she wanted a White man for a husband. He knew Levi was worthy of her love, though. He was secretly happy for them both, but he had to show a stern face in front of his warriors. Sometimes they were like children with their bickering and woman chasing. Too much so for their own good.

When Dahteste and Levi sat before the chief, he asked, "Do you know what Dahteste means?"

"She told me it means Warrior Woman," Levi replied.

"And do you know who gave you that name?" he asked Dahteste.

"My father gave me the name, didn't he?" she replied, now unsure of herself. The chief looked at her with piercing eyes like he could see what she was thinking.

Hachta locked eyes with Dahteste and said, "I told your father to give you your name. I knew you would be a warrior from your fifth summer. On your tenth summer, I knew you would be a warrior chief. This is how things are. At the time, it was best some didn't know how close I was to your father and eventually to you. I am like an uncle to you, but I have always given you your space and allowed you to live alone—even the freedom to learn alone. Do you think you would have been groomed for a warrior if I didn't order it?" He smiled, flashing white teeth. "There are always too many willing young men who want to hold the honor of warrior, not alone warrior chief. We have always known who you were—even before you did."

The chief smiled, took Dahteste's hand, and pulled her to her feet. She looked into the chief's deep gray smoldering eyes. Hachta put his arms around her, and she put her head against his chest. When she lifted her head, they locked eyes again. Hers were slightly glazed, and a single tear cut a streak down her cherry-red cheeks. She stared at him, and he winked as he cocked his head quizzically. His eyes danced with playfulness. He was enjoying himself.

Hachta looked at Levi and said, "Come and sit beside me with your new wife. We must talk. You do know you are not marrying a normal woman, don't you? You are marrying the woman warrior and a war chief. She has an honorable place in our tribe, and you will be respected as she is. I have only heard good things about you, Levi Beaver Johnson. Dahteste is like my lost daughter brought back from the dead, and you will be like my son."

Of course, Chief Hachta spoke in Crow so his people could understand. A murmur rippled through the crowd, and some gasped at what was said. A few of the warrior braves huffed in anger. Not everybody was happy about what was happening, but the vast majority always favored what their chief decided. He was wiser than them, and he had repeatedly proved it. Nobody had the audacity to speak out against him. Not even the warriors who had fancied Dahteste for their wife. Now it was clear that was not meant to be.

They were also getting their first look at Levi Beaver Johnson up close; he towered over every man in the camp and was half again as broad. His long blond hair and beard made him stand out in the Indian camp full of black hair and dark, beardless faces.

Angus translated for the rest of the mountain men. While everyone was drawn to the chief, Pine Needle popped up from the crowd, grabbed Angus, and nearly tore him away. She wore a wicked smile, and her eyes were full of mischief.

"Hold your horses, woman," Angus grumbled. "Shush, now. I've got to hear what Chief Hachta says. Dennis only knows enough Crow to keep from gettin' shot. My Pine Needle taught me, and as you can see, Levi learns the native languages as fast as he's learned everything else. The man is a one-of-a-kind, and I got a feelin' his new bride is one-of-a-kind too."

Chief Hachta looked at Levi and said, "What I won't allow you to do is live with this White man until you are married. It is only fitting for a war chief to make an example for those younger men and women who want to follow in your footsteps. Maybe one day your new husband will become a Crow warrior too." He stared at Levi. He felt like he was looking into his soul. Finally, the chief smiled.

So many tribe members gasped that everybody heard it. The chief knew he was saying things that would shock his people, but he wanted to get this over with and settled before one of his warriors challenged Dahteste new husband to a fight to the death. He did not doubt that his warrior would die, and he couldn't afford to lose any more men nor allow his men to take on an impossible opponent and lose face themselves.

This way, he was gaining one of the best White warriors he had seen besides Rusty Steel, and he was like a brother. He also understood the value of having Levi in his tribe, not only for a source of trading but his superior skills in trapping beaver and fish. They had observed him from afar.

That was how they found his first discovery of the

streams and ponds full of beaver so close, and still, nobody ever discovered the spot but the young mountain man. Of course, the chief never imagined Dahteste would fall in love with Johnson, but now that he saw them together, they were so alike they were like grains of corn on a cob. They fit together perfectly; he saw they were always meant to be. He just didn't see it.

The chief raised his hand, and the drums started again. Several men dressed in fancy feather headdresses danced, pounding their feet to the beat of the drums and song. All the tribe chanted together, then an elder stood, and they went silent. Then he began to tell the story of the bride-to-be.

Dahteste looked into Levi's eyes and smiled.

Levi leaned over and whispered in her ear, "I'll be happy to be your rubican."

Dahteste looked at him, puzzled, and Levi laughed. "I'll tell ya later, darlin'. Why do you think the chief didn't wait for Rusty Steel?"

"Oh, I'm sure he had a reason," Dahteste said. "He never does anything without making it part of his big plan.

"Big plan?" Levi asked. "And what's that supposed to mean?"

She laughed and replied, "Your guess is as good as mine."

Levi Johnson felt like he had left Earth and landed in another universe. He had just gotten his first look at Indian life from the other side of the spectrum. Now he saw everything through Dahteste's eyes, and everyone appeared different. He wondered if this was his destiny. Would he feel at home living in the Crow stronghold or long for the cabin and his friends? It was clear the chief planned to marry them. He wondered how it would have gone if Levi didn't want to marry her. Lucky for him, he was head-over-heels and wanted nothing more than to be with his soon-to-be Crow bride even though the marrying part had been planned for next spring.

He didn't have it clear how things had changed from that very morning. They had planned to live in their tipi. Levi wondered if it was still there or if the chief had also brought it to the stronghold. They had intended to return to the camp when the weather got warmer, get married, and then go back to stay in the compound. Now it looked like Chief Hachta wanted him to be a member of his tribe, which would mean living with the Crow Indians. He wondered how he would adapt. Maybe it wouldn't be any different than he lived now with Dahteste, except he would have a wife.

Yet he would be surrounded by a hundred tipis and hundreds of Crow men, women, and children, and he was used to living with a few friends in their little compound lost in the mountains. He had hoped to spend the winter with nothing to do but get to know Dahteste, but that wasn't meant to be. He wished Rusty Steel was there to help him with what to do. He never realized until right then how much he had learned from him and how much more he had to learn, whether it be from Rusty or somebody else.

Or maybe his time to teach the young mountain man had come to an end, and he ran out of things to teach Levi Beaver Johnson. Rusty's always said one of his best lessons in life was living with the American Indians. Maybe it was time for Levi to turn to this type of life if for nothing else, to give it a chance.

He wondered what Will Forrester, his best friend,

thought about all this. As it was, Levi didn't even know what he thought about it all yet. It didn't matter anyway because whatever the chief had planned for him, he had to comply or put all of them in danger and stand the chance of losing Dahteste. That was something he never wanted to do. He was in love for the first time. Then again, he hadn't ever been around many women other than his mother. In southeastern Indiana, there weren't hordes of women to choose from. Not in the wilderness.

And his journey across the west and Kansas had been so hair-raising that he never had time to think about women. He had the wilderness on his mind, and fate made him bump into Dahteste; it was simple as that. Levi felt it was obvious that it was meant to be. Only fate could bring two people together in such a way. He looked at Dahteste, and her big brown eyes twinkled in delight as she batted her long eyelashes.

"It didn't turn out that bad, did it now?" Levi laughed.

He looked over at his friends. Angus had already disappeared with Pine Needle, and the rest of the boys were eating the feast with the rest of the tribe's members. The drums continued to hammer through the day. When the sun began to drop off the edge of the earth, the sky turned a fire red. It was ominous and looked like the end of the world. But everybody in the Crow camp was happy, dancing. The elders sang songs of heroes and martyrs of times past, and the chief told stories.

Levi found he could understand nearly everything. He had never tried to speak a language other than English, and he hadn't found it difficult, which surprised him. When he left Indiana, he was an expert shot and trapper. Now he was a true frontiersman and was just about to be drummed into the Crow tribe. Since he had no control over what was happening, he let it wash over him like an ocean wave.

FLATHEAD INDIANS

DURING THE DAY, A BRIGHT FIRE ROARED IN THE CAVE from dawn till dusk. Rusty kept it stoked with wood. There must have been some small opening deep inside somewhere because the smoke disappeared into the black mouth like a draft in a chimney. This was lucky for Rusty, so he could warm the cave walls during the day without leaving a trail of smoke in the sky indicating exactly where he was. It also helped keep the warmth in, but not if the temperatures dropped dramatically. The fire kept them warm in the daytime, but when it got really cold was at night, and he just couldn't risk it. The cave's opening glowed like a beacon in the dark, and there were Indians close by.

Still, he had yet to determine the tribe and the actual number. He had only heard three voices. Then again, there weren't many Indians anywhere that liked White men except maybe the Cherokee back east. He had to assume they were hostile. He believed he could still handle three men in one go if he had to. There was a time when he wouldn't have even questioned such a thing, but time seemed to be passing by quicker than he realized, and suddenly, he noticed his hair was gray, as was his beard. Spots appeared on the tops of his hands, and he had a few new wrinkles. Since he hardly ever shaved sometimes, he went six months without looking in a mirror. Ten years ago, when he got up in the morning, he was full of spunk and vinegar right off the bat. Now it took him two or three coffees to get him moving and into gear.

Rusty looked at Dog and said, "Old age is comin' for me at a really bad time, my new friend."

The dog cocked its head and looked questioningly.

Outside, the wind began to blow early that morning, and it was snowing again by noon. This time it came down in earnest. Tonight, the temperatures will drop well below freezing. Rusty could already feel it in his bones. If it weren't for the three Indians he spotted trapping, he could build a fire all night long like he had been doing, but now that he knew they were near, he didn't dare take the chance. He had fetched his good bedroll and extra bearskin from his dead mule and prepared for a stormy night.

Rusty crawled to the entrance on his hands and knees. As he peered out, the snow came down at a steep angle. When he stuck his head out and stood, icy wind peppered his face, making his cheeks sting. He used his snowshoes like shovels to scrape the layer of power away and look for stones on the ground. As he gathered rocks the size of his fist, he stacked them at the cave's entrance. While working, he watched for any motion, noise, or smell. He knew the warriors were close. He ensured his pistols and rifles were primed, the powder was dry, and they were within reach. He might have to defend himself at any moment. Hopefully, they wouldn't find the cave.

He crawled back in when he had a large pile of rocks by the door. Rusty carried the stones from the entrance to the fire, setting them all around the cinders and some right in the flames. He ducked outside for more dead wood. It was a good thing a lightning-struck tree stood beside the cave in various states of decomposition. It supplied him with all the wood he needed. By the end of the day, he had fiery hot rocks the size of softballs stacked high beside the fire. Then he dug out a space about six inches deep, the size of his bedroll.

Before it got dark, he lined the bottom with hot rocks. When he was done, he covered them with dirt and laid his bedroll on top. The warm stones guaranteed he would survive the freezing night to come. He might be aging and wounded, but he still had a trick or two up his sleeve. He chuckled, and the dog looked again, puzzled.

Rusty sat at the low entrance and watched as the sun set on jagged cliffs to his west. He looked up at the last vestiges of light and watched as the snow fell so thick it became a whiteout just before sunset. Rusty crawled back into the dark cave and felt around for his bed. The glow of embers still shone in the room, so he could just make out what he was doing. He pulled a candle from his bag and lit it as he pulled out his ceramic pipe and a twist of tobacco, as he had his nightly read. Tonight, he had a penny dreadful about a crime mystery named *The Bradys and the Fire Marshal*.

He pulled the book out of his large frontiersman's pocket in his buckskin shirt, poured coffee into his cup, and gobbled the hot liquid down to prepare him for the night. The wind howled outside, but he was as warm as toast in the cave, but he knew by morning it would be an icebox. He would sleep warm from the heated rocks under his bed, though. It was a trick the leader of the Crow tribe showed him where he had lived a decade before. Now that the night cold had a solution, he knew at first light he could make another fire without risking being discovered, warming the cave again.

As he dozed off, he felt when Dog lay down on his warm bedroll. It groaned as it lay down. Rusty pulled the buffalo robe over his new friend. His new dog breathed out a deep, long sigh and closed its eyes. It nuzzled its head into Rusty's hip and fell asleep. In minutes both man and dog were snoring softy.

Bats fluttered above them, and a few even tried to venture into the blizzard, but they returned as quickly as they left. They silently fluttered their wings until they settled down in the dark, waiting for the storm to pass so they could go out and hunt for food. The wind blew so hard that a snow drift formed at the entrance making it even more challenging to see.

Rusty dreamed of faraway places. At first, he was a young captain on the river again, but Dog was with him. Sometimes he looked back and thought it was there, but it was only his shadow. He saw his ship go up in flames as the wheelhouse toppled into the water. He remembered the swim across the river and his flee to safety—something he couldn't say for his first mate and deckhands. He shook his head, and beads of sweat popped up on his brow. His eyes darted around under his eyelids like a bolt of electricity hit them.

He awoke with a start and sat suddenly, startling the dog. It growled deeply but looked around and went back to sleep. The coals in the fire had gone cold hours before, and the stone walls had turned cold. It was black in the cave, so he didn't move from his bed and had no fire to light the candle. He lay there and looked up into the dark, where he knew hundreds of bats were hanging. Still, he could hear the wind howl. It was much stronger than when he went to bed. He thanked his lucky star that the dog had such an excellent den to share with his human friend.

He couldn't sleep a wink more that night. His mind kept going back to the three Indians he heard talk. Then it hit him. He had heard that language years ago. It was Flathead. They sometimes traded with the Crow when they weren't enemies. Now he can remember back some fifteen years. A few came to barter for coffee and tobacco. He remembered how strange their language sounded compared to Crow, to which he had become accustomed.

Rusty Steel lay and waited until the first light showed in the mouth of the cave. In half an hour, he could build his fire again. Then he would have to decide what to do with the Indians. He knew they wouldn't believe there was room on this mountain for the four of them. He still wasn't sure there weren't more. Nor did he know if they were proper Flathead hunters or were they warrior braves. That small detail could make all the difference in the world. He would rather fight hunters than warriors any day.

———

THE FLATHEAD INDIANS had just returned to their makeshift camp and built a fire in their shelter. Still, the temperatures were dropping like a rock in a pond. But they had lived in cold conditions before and knew how to keep warm. They huddled over the fire, trying to warm themselves after a spell out.

"A blizzard is on its way," White Feather said. "It's time to take our beaver down and out of the mountains. We can cure them over the winter; when the Rendezvous arrives, we will have enough money to buy three rifles.

"How many beaver pelts does it cost for one rifle?" Raven asked.

"I don't know, but we must have enough," White Feather said. "I've heard Crow say they pay twelve to thirteen cold-water pelts for a single rifle, but I've heard of a Blackfoot trading for twenty."

"You'd have to be crazy to sell a Blackfoot Indian a rifle," Raven said. "He might turn around and shoot you with it."

"The White men will cheat us anyway," Blue Face said. "Maybe we can trade for the rifles and later come and steal them back." He grinned.

"If they cheat us, we will kill them," Raven spat. "I'll be happy to kill my first White man."

"I thought we were concentrating on trapping and earning enough for rifles," White Feather said. "Now, all of a sudden, you want to kill White men in the meet no less. It's dangerous business messing with the White men who live in the Rocky Mountains. Most of the men at the Rendezvous are mountain men. They're crack shots with their rifles, and we're only armed with bows, arrows, and lances."

"I'm not afraid," Raven growled as he puffed out his chest.

"Yes, and with that attitude, soon you'll be dead," White Feather said. "If we kill someone, what do you think the five hundred White people attending the fur trading meet will do? They will cut us up and burn our flesh so only our dust is left. Then we will never make it to the spirit world. Young braves always manage to get into trouble no matter where they go. A smart warrior always goes undetected and only shows himself if he wants."

"Get the fire going," Blue Face said. "I'm freezing, and you know as well as I do, you're the only warrior of the three of us, and even you haven't killed a White man. Have you ever killed a Blackfoot—or maybe a Crow Indian?"

"Stop," White Feather said. "Do you smell the smoke too?"

All three Indians closed their eyes and took in deep breaths.

"They're close," White Feather whispered. "Someone's made a fire. Who could be up here with us?"

"Why don't we just get our furs and leave first thing in the morning," Blue Face said. "We have enough furs to trade for three rifles. Plus, the cold winter is on top of us. If we leave tomorrow, we might just get away."

"And what if somebody sees our fire tonight?" White Feather asked. "We won't survive without a fire, so we must find the source of the smoke before it's dark. It is too late to flee anyway. The blizzard is on us already. By nightfall, we won't be able to see. We've also got to consider we may have already been discovered. We have to go on the offensive to be safe. Leave the beaver, and let's try to see if we can follow the smell of burning wood."

"But it's snowing too hard," Blue Face said. "If it gets worse, we might lose our way; then we'll lose our lives."

"I'm not a coward," Raven spat. "Not like some people I know." He eyed Blue Face, but neither one was a warrior. The problem was Raven wanted to be a warrior and was trying to use White Feather as his sponsor. But if he wasn't up to the mark, the person who vouched for him would be in trouble too.

"Since when is saving your life a cowardly way?" Blue Face asked. "The wise man steals away into the night and picks a better time to engage. Not during a blizzard."

"How do you know a blizzard is coming anyway?" Raven spat. "It's just more snow. It's been snowing off and on for weeks."

"To freeze to death is not an honorable way to die," Blue Face said. He pulled his bearskin robe up around his ears and held his hands over the fire.

"Nobody is going to die," White Feather growled. "Shut up, and let's go find out where the smoke is coming from. That will decide what we do or don't do. And don't talk so loud. We don't want to stumble into an enemy camp like three buffalo."

"Shut up and act like a warrior brave for once," Raven growled, but he could hardly hide his grin. He was a wannabe warrior who harassed Blue Face to gain White Feather's attention, but he wasn't impressed with his hunting partners. He should have brought a couple of warrior braves with him. Then the only danger is when they rode off to challenge some warrior from another tribe or a White man. It was hard to keep a warrior's attention focused on hunting when there were other Indians to fight."

"We can deal with the White men after we have our rifles," White Feather said. "Then we will have the same advantages as they do. It shouldn't take long to learn how they work."

"What can be complicated?" Raven asked. "It's just like pointing a stick."

The three Flathead Indians followed their noses across the valley and up the adjoining mountain and began to climb. When they were halfway up, they saw a sliver of smoke coming from a crack in the snow. The closer they got, the stronger it smelled of campfire. They scoured the land before them, but they didn't see any movement for a mile. They drew their arrows back in their bows and stealth fully closed in on the source of the smoke.

White Feather walked right up to the faint trail of smoke. It smelled of dry wood and came from a crack in the stone. He brushed away the snow, but he couldn't even see inside. It was as black as night, and the crack was so small he could hardly get the flat of his hand inside. He wondered where the other end of the cave was. It must be big enough for a man to enter. Otherwise, there wouldn't be a fire on the other end.

"We've got to find the entrance to this cave," White Feather whispered. "They're so close we can smell them."

All three Indians had another look around, but they didn't see a thing, yet the smell of burning wood was strong in the air.

"We're going to have to climb the mountain and go down the other side to see if we can't find the opening," White Feather said. "It should be easier to see at night."

Blue Face looked up the steep trail and said, "That's a long way up there."

"Stop acting like a fool and get moving," White Feather snapped.

"And who made you the leader of our war party?" Raven asked.

"I thought we were a hunting party," Blue Face said. "I came to trap beaver, not challenge Blackfeet Indians."

"How do you know they're Blackfeet Indians?" Raven asked. "Keep your mouth shut and save yourself the dishonor."

"Because there are more Blackfoot Indians around here than there are Ute or Crow," Blue Face said. "Why I doubt there be more Flatheads than us right now. I'd rather fight a Ute war party than three Blackfeet."

"How would you know?" Raven asked. "You've never fought a Blackfoot Indian."

"Neither have you, fool," Blue Face retorted.

VICTORY TO THE VICTOR

WHEN MORNING CAME, THE THREE FLATHEAD INDIANS were all bundled together, using their body heat to keep from freezing. They let the fire burn all night, and nobody showed up. At least they hoped that nobody saw them. The first thing they did was make some White man's coffee—that and tobacco. Many of the Indians in the wilderness had discovered such things as coffee, tobacco twists, peppermint, and all the fancy colorful beads they could want.

They all knew it was important to leave open paths to trade with the White settlers even if they didn't like them on their land. A thing as simple as a steel knife could change their lives. They needed metal tools to do almost everything, not to mention sewing needles and fishhooks. Even mirrors were a treasure to many Indians—especially the women who all wanted to be beautiful for their men and family.

"Quick, make the coffee," Raven nagged at Blue Face. "And put some more wood on the fire." He looked down at him, scowling. "You aren't good for anything."

As a baby, Blue Face nearly died from lack of oxygen at birth. His face turned blue and stayed that way for most of his childhood, but the name stuck for life. White Feather was given his name when he became a warrior, and Raven got his name for his dark thoughts. He had never killed a man but bragged about his skills unceasingly. Men who had really been in battle recognized the type instantly.

He had yet to prove his mettle. Usually, the ones with the biggest mouths were the most afraid. Just like an Indian camp dog. The ones that are afraid barked the most. Time would tell if Raven was presented with the opportunity to show his bravery, or would he stand up to the challenge like a man, or would he fold and run?

White Feather didn't like spending the winter with two hunters, even if they were Flathead Indians like himself. He was only interested in the rifle. The mere position would make him a more important warrior. He wondered if it was difficult to use. It appeared as easy as pointing a finger. He was a warrior, and they didn't even know how to treat him. Often, they said things that offended him, but they didn't even realize what they had done.

He suspected that Raven wasn't as dangerous and daring as he claimed. Any men who talked about how they could kill and injure like he did had probably never done either. He watched and waited to see what happened. Hopefully, they would not be put to the test. The last thing he wanted was to find other Indians and have to fight with two men who had never fought for their lives. He wouldn't have anybody to cover his back.

They sat and drank their coffee; then they headed out in the direction where they discovered the smoke seeping from the crack in the rock. Maybe it was a Ute or Blackfoot hunting or trapping party, and they had pulled up stakes and left. It was apparent the weather was just about to get worse. But for a warrior, weather was never enough to stop him once he was on the trail of his prey.

"All we have to do is go over that mountain and down the other side," White Feather whispered. "The fire has to be coming from there. Be careful where you step, and make sure you don't make any loud noises. We don't want to alarm whoever it is making that fire. We have to find out, or we can't stay another night. If they're warriors, they may kill us in our sleep."

"Why don't we turn back and leave now while we can?" Blue Face asked. His eyes stretched wide, and beads of sweat covered his face. "That's a long way up there, and then we've got to come back and get our things. We'll have to climb that mountain twice."

"It's either find out who's making that fire or stand a chance of getting our scalps taken tonight, fool," White Feather said. "Listen to what I tell you and save your breath. You talk entirely too much."

"What have I been saying?" Raven said. "We should leave him behind. We don't need him anyway."

"You shut your trap too, moron," White Feather growled. "You're both are as dumb as two rocks in a sack. Now be quiet and follow me and try to keep up. We want to make it there and back before dark. If not, we'll have no place to shelter."

Blue Face was quiet for the rest of the morning, but

he didn't like where they were going. Hunters usually took the route with the least resistance. The warriors looked for trouble. He knew when he agreed to go with White Feather it was dodgy, and he was stepping out of his league. Every time hunters paired up with warrior braves, somebody got killed. He didn't want to be that next somebody.

Hopefully, it won't be me, Blue Face thought. He wondered what he would do when he faced the enemy, which now seemed inevitable. He had never even considered fighting enemy warriors. He had always focused on feeding the hungry mouths of the tribe's members. Maybe the warriors looked down on them, but without food, they would have to tribe to protect.

His heart pounded between his ears as they led the horses up the steep trails. It took them nearly four hours to reach the top, and White Feather nearly ran. Blue Face pushed himself to his limits to save face, but when he arrived at the summit, he was worn out. As a hunter, he was used to moving through the wilderness slowly and quietly, carefully making sure not to scare his prey. Now they were hunting something that fought back and moving faster through the wilderness than he had ever gone. He wondered what tribe they would be from.

What does it matter who they are? Blue Face thought.

When they got to the top, they stopped to rest. Raven and Blue Face both struggled to gobble up enough air. They both felt faint, but White Feather was ready to go again. He seemed to be made of something different than the other two. He never seemed to tire and had no apparent fear. His confidence was the only reason they continued to follow. Even Raven struggled to stand, and White Feather had already begun to descend. His horse's footing slipped behind him, but he never looked back.

"Why take the horses down the mountain and back up again?" Blue Face asked. "It makes no sense. And if one falls, we will go down the mountain with it. The trail is slippery with snow."

Raven hemmed and hawed as he stalled but couldn't see a reason not to. Of course, White Feather saw visions of himself riding into battle at full charge, bashing in the heads of his enemies with his tomahawks. He carried one on either side, a bow and quiver of arrows across his back, and a lance in his hand. He had worked all his life for these moments. There were no moments that Blue Face cherished. He would rather be bringing back a big fat elk to the tribe for a feast. When he arrived home, the members of the tribe always celebrated. With the warrior always came celebration too, but it also brought pain and suffering for the wives, fathers and mothers, and fatherless children.

Raven nodded, tied his horse to a tree stump, and hobbled it as the hunter did. Then they began the steep climb down the hill. They slipped and slid down, making the distance in half the time they climbed up. Soon they had the small opening sighted. It was only large enough for a man to enter on all fours. They had found their mystery man. White Feather was nearly at the entrance to the small cave.

"Wait for us," Blue Face said as loud as he dared.

When the black furry animal lunged out of the snow, the Flathead warrior was caught totally by surprise. The long white canine teeth sunk deep into the skin, scraping bone, and finally snapping the tibia. It sounded like a dried tree branch breaking. The warrior brave screamed so loud the veins in his neck popped out, and veins pulsated at his temple. The dog suddenly let loose, sank its teeth into his arm, and began shaking him like a rag doll.

Raven was horrified at what he saw. He was ready for a confrontation with some enemy tribe or other. But the last thing he expected was for a massive wolf to pounce on their leader and began tearing him to pieces.

When the arrow pierced Raven's chest, you could hear the thud. The flinthead arrow traversed his chest, ribs, lung, and heart. Blood gushed from his mouth. He didn't even see the man who killed him. He wondered what tribe they came from. He fell to the ground, and a cloud of red snow spread around him.

The mountain man popped up out of the snow just like the giant dog, but he had a bow in his hands. A second arrow was already strung and ready to let fly. Blue Face's mouth opened and closed like a beached fish. His eyes were spread so wide they looked like they were about to pop out of his head. His mouth turned so dry his lips stuck to his front teeth. Despite the cold, beads of sweat ran down his face.

They locked eyes, and Rusty asked in Crow, "Are you Flathead?"

Blue Face nodded and frowned. They hadn't even known the white man was there. He never imagined Flathead Indians being caught out by a single White man. He began to sing his death song as he raised his hands, palms up, and chanted while looking at the sky. He could hear the dog finally let go of White Feather.

He suddenly felt a burst of courage. It was the last thing he expected. His mouth turned into a hard line, and his eyes looked like flint. This man had killed his fellow Flathead, and he had to seek restitution even if it meant losing his life doing it. He spun on his heels and threw the knife. The blade flashed as it tumbled toward its target and Blue Face charged.

SPRING

WHEN THE MOUNTAIN MEN RETURNED TO THE COMPOUND, they did so without Dahteste and Levi Johnson. Both had been expected to stay in the new tipi the tribe had constructed for her and her husband. If they ran off, they would show a lack of respect which they didn't want to do. Both had expected the welcome to be unfriendly, but it couldn't be farther from the truth. In the end, all the worrying was for nothing.

Angus, Will, Dennis, Bob, and Sam really expected Rusty Steel to already be back there and waiting for them, but there wasn't anybody there. The whole way home, Angus searched the treetops for signs of smoke signals. He expected him to require help. But there were no floating messages in the sky. He didn't even know which way to look. He could be in trouble, and they had no way of helping him.

Then when they neared the compound, they expected to see smoke coming from their cabin's chimneys, but the sky was clear and crisp without a sign of a single trace of smoke. He looked up again and searched for vultures. He had to shake his head to push the thoughts out of his mind and try to think positively.

Angus was visibly shaken when they stepped into the compound. The snow was virgin and was void of footprints. The trail to the outhouse was covered in snow, and there were drifts on both the water closet and the front door and porch of Angus and Rusty's cabin. It hadn't been disturbed.

"I knew my gut feelin' was right all along," Angus huffed. His brow furrowed, and his eyes narrowed. "What are we gonna do? I ain't up to goin' out and taking a chance of getting caught in a blizzard. I don't think I'd weather it well at my age."

"I'll go," Forrester said. "If I'm fast, I might find him."

"We don't even have a direction to go in," Angus huffed. "When Rusty left, he made it a point of not saying where he was goin'. As a matter of fact, he didn't mention when he'd be back either. Oh, sure, it ain't all that unusual for one of us to wander off, but not this time of year and not for so long. He don't even have anywhere to stay if the weather gets bad."

Mountain Dennis lay his hand on Forrester's shoulder and said, "You can't go out there, son. I wouldn't even send Levi to go out now. I'm afraid it's too late in the season to travel. We'll just have to let old Rusty work it out on his own. From here to spring, there ain't nowhere to go. Get some of that firewood Levi chopped up, and let's get these fireplaces lit up." He looked at the sky. "There's gonna be a doozy comin' in tonight. I hope to heavens Rusty has somewhere warm to stay."

Just like Angus said, that night, the temperatures dropped, the wind rose, and snow fell in abundance.

The wind whistled through the trees around the cabin. They could see the rope to the outhouse swing in the wind through the window with the last vestiges of light.

"Be a good lad and put on a couple more logs, Will," Angus whispered. "This one's gonna be a humdinger."

———————

FOUR MONTHS HAD PASSED, and the winter's first blizzard proved to be the worst. Most Indians suffered because their homes weren't as warm as some, and the gusts of wind blew others away. Back in the compound, all six mountain men worked around the table in Angus's cabin. The fire roared, sending black smoke snaking up and out the chimney that poked out of the sod roof. Heat waves rippled across the room, making it as warm as freshly baked bread. A jug of corn liquor sat at the center of the table as the men around it worked their beaver hides.

The sun was just setting, and Angus walked to the window like he had been doing all winter and looked out. The windowpane was blurry, so he used his shirt-sleeve to clear the steam and condensation—still no signs of a single track. Levi had even come and gone twice with his wife, and they hadn't heard a thing in the Indian gossip. If something happened on this side of the mountain, they would have heard one way or the other. If he had traveled beyond country that they knew, anything could have happened.

That night Angus went to sleep with a heavy heart. He felt it in his bones that something had happened to his best friend, Rusty. Good weather had arrived, and Steel hadn't. He and Forrester closed up once the rest of the mountain men headed for their cabins. They stoked the fire, but the temperatures were already getting better. Some of the snow would start to melt in a couple of months, and they would nearly be in summer. Before Angus blew the kerosene lantern out, he had one last glimpse in the moonlit night for his old friend. A silver tint shone across the mountains.

Early the next morning, Angus heard a familiar snoring before the sun rose. He blinked his eyes open as he smiled. He looked over at Rusty's bunk and was surprised to see the biggest dog he had ever seen sleeping beneath his cot. Both seemed to be resting in peace. Angus smiled and wobbled his head as he silently got up, stifling a chuckle. He started the cookfire and made frying pan biscuits and strips of fried bacon. He even made some cornbread with their corn flour stock. Soon Rusty was rubbing his eyes with his fists and sniffing the air. He swung his feet onto the cold floor and sighed. When he looked at Angus, a new life danced in his eyes. He seemed five years younger.

"Where in the world have you been, fool?" Angus grumbled. "I was just about to rent out your cot. Then where would you have to go?"

Even though he had been looking for Rusty every day for months, suddenly, he felt angry that nothing had happened to him. Everybody in the compound was worried. The only one who said he would come when he was ready was his good friend Crow Chief Hachta. Somehow, he knew how Rusty felt. They were the same age, and both men were too proud for their own good too, but they were still good, honest men.

"What do you care where I've been," Rusty retorted. "You ain't my boss. I don't have to answer to you or anybody for that matter." He wobbled his head in defiance.

"You've been up to your old tricks again, ain't cha," Angus said as he eyed his old friend. "Runnin' off to God knows where and doin' who knows what. And now you show up with a mutt."

"That ain't no mutt," Rusty growled. "He's a danged sight smarter than you."

"And what's his name, iffin, you don't mind I ask?"

"Dog," Rusty replied, all a matter of fact like.

"Dog?" Angus asked. "Whatcha mean, dog? What kind of name is that for whatever that thing is you call a canine?"

Forrester was just sitting up in his cot. He smiled when he heard the familiar banter between his two old friends. He watched them bicker. It made him grin like a possum. He too was happy to see Rusty was back and alive and kicking.

"Howdy, Rusty," Will said. "It's good to see you're still in one piece."

"Well, at least somebody's happy to see me," Rusty replied, but he winked and smiled at Forrester when Angus wasn't looking.

Later that day, Levi and Dahteste stopped by to see if the compound boys had heard anything from Rusty Steel. At this point, even Hachta was getting worried and told Levi if he wasn't back, he would send a war party out to get him. Despite the scare, it seemed like everything had gotten right back to normal as soon as Rusty arrived.

"Pour a little of that whiskey into my coffee," Rusty said and smiled.

Forrester poured coffee for them all.

"Why don't you give that poor dog a decent name?" Angus grumbled. "You can't name that mut, Dog, for Pete's sake. I just can't get used to such a thing. I don't call my mule, Jackass, do I?"

"First of all, I reckon I can call Dog any danged thing I wanna," Rusty retorted. "How do we know he don't have a proper name already? He might understand every word we're sayin' right now. I don't want to confuse the poor animal, either. You do know that d-o-g is God spelled backward, don't cha? I reckon the canines have a special place in Heaven, just like us mountain men, or at least I hope so. Why would they have such a name if not?"

Dahteste whispered into Levi's ear, "Do they always fight? I don't understand all the words, but I can see their faces."

Levi smiled and said, "Look at their eyes, darlin'. There you can see how they really feel. They're just grumpy because they're getting on in years and think they be old. Angus may be on in age, but I figure Rusty Steel has a good decade in front of him if he just lets go and ages like a gentleman."

"Gentleman?" Dahteste asked. "I don't know that word."

Levi laughed a deep, happy laugh. "We don't use that word around here all that much. Oh, I reckon we all be gentlemen all right, at least in as far as women folk. Especially the captain. He's what they call a gentleman and a scholar, and Angus says I'm one-of-a-kind, but I ain't figured out iffin that's good or not yet."

"Spot's a good name for a mutt," Angus said, just as stubborn as always. "There's no way I'm gonna call a dog, Dog. It don't even sound right when I say it."

"First of all, there ain't a single spot on 'im," Rusty growled. "Just because we live in the same house don't mean you can boss me around. I'll call the dog Dirt iffin I wanna."

"There ya go offendin' your own animal," Angus huffed. "You call 'im what cha want, but I'm gonna call 'im somethin' else. I just don't know what that is yet. Names are for keeps, for heaven's sake. We have to choose carefully, or the name might not suit 'im."

"Whatcha mean, *we* gotta?" Rusty spat. "There ain't no *we* in it. I didn't see you bring my dog into camp. This here animal fought off a mountain lion to save me."

"To save you? I thought you said nothin' happened on your venture into the winter." Angus snickered. "I knew it wasn't a walk in the park like you said it was. Now that we know something's happened, do you wanna tell us?"

"It wasn't nothin' Dog, and me couldn't take care of on your own," Rusty huffed, aloof. "I can survive on my own even in the wilderness just like I've been doin' from ever since I was a wharf rat."

"So, iffin, your canine saved your life from a mountain lion; where's the skin?" Angus asked with raised eyebrows. He knew he was gettin' under Rusty's skin, but he also knew he'd do the same to him. "Come on, spit it out. You know there ain't no secrets in these mountains. Somebody was probably watchin' ya anyway. You know how the Crow be."

"I reckon every Crow Indian in the Rockies was at the wedding," Rusty growled. "I still don't know why Hachta didn't wait on me. Maybe we ain't as good of friends as I thought. If y'all had a pow-wow without me, why should I tell ya what I was up to in the wilderness?"

"It must have been somethin' awful bad iffin ya don't wanna talk about it." Angus chuckled. "That's fine. I know it wasn't all roses and glory. But iffin, you don't wanna tell us, we don't have to tell you about the party."

"And why would I care about a dad-gummed party at my age," Rusty growled.

"Anything else ya wanna talk about, fool?" Angus asked. He couldn't hold back the grin. "I can smell the wood a-burnin'. I knew you were up to your old shenanigans. I can tell by that new scar on you face. What'd ya do? Run into a late grizzly or a big cat?"

Dahteste curled her legs up on her bearskin and faced Levi, gently shifting her weight to near her face to his. She lay her head on his shoulder; she looked at Rusty.

"We wanted you to be there," Dahteste said in Crow. She understood just enough English to know what Rusty was saying. "It was a wise decision that Chief Hachta made. There were some unhappy warriors because I ran off with Levi. It was to keep them from trying to kill him—or Levi from killing them. You know how men get about women. I have no idea why they got the idea they owned me and could make up my mind for me. Especially with me being a war chief."

"Some men be like that," Angus said, "but they ain't gentlemen like us."

"Gentlemen," Dahteste repeated. "I like that word."

"It's a word rarely used in the Rocky Mountains," Rusty said, happy they had stopped talking about him. "You should thank your lucky stars; such a bunch of men surrounds you."

Rusty wanted his experience to be for him only. It wasn't a big thing, but it was his thing. He smiled knowingly as he scratched Dog's head. He had proved he was still up to living in the wilderness and proved it to the only important person. He proved it to himself. He smiled—he wasn't even listening to what Angus complained about. Let him ask all the questions he wanted to.

Rusty was happy to keep his secret. Why let them even think he had gone out with doubts about his skills? He had spent a winter roughing it and survived, and it had been as difficult as hell. That was all his friends had to know. That he was still up to whatever was thrown at him. He even saved a man's life and let the last Flathead Indian go. He was one of the bravest men he had ever seen.

UNFORGOTTEN

LEVI JOHNSON MOUNTAIN MAN
SCOUT 10

This is dedicated to my mother; may she rest in peace.
Sadly, she never got to read my work.

"You have to die a couple of times
before you actually live."

Charles Bukowski

BLAZE

THE CLOPPING OF HORSE'S HOOVES ECHOED IN THE forest. Ex-Captain Will Forrester rode alone through the wilderness. Pine, spruce, and ferns towered over the rider as their scents floated in the air. He crossed a green valley with the first traces of buffalo tracks. He pulled his hat down to shade his eyes. Spring was in full bloom, and most of the snow in the valleys had turned from white blankets to lush green carpets. White-tailed ptarmigan, blue grouse, Clark's nutcracker, western tanager, and mountain chickadees had just arrived from migration. Birds chattered as they jumped from limb to limb.

Three-toed woodpeckers tapped their beaks against the trees as crows cawed from their perches, mocking the intruder. Vultures made lazy circles in the sky, waiting for something to die. Eagles and hawks soared, looking for a live meal. A moose bellowed and barked somewhere in the next valley. Its echo bounced off the canyon's walls.

A mountain lion roared somewhere high in the

forest. A chill ran up Forrester's back, and goose bumps sprouted on his arms. The weather was warm, and the mountains were noisy with game. As he moved forward, he kept his eyes peeled for danger—something inherent to the Rocky Mountains.

The white stallion stomped its hooves as it pranced across the flats. A US Army brand moved on its muscular rump. The man riding the majestic animal wore buckskins with Army-issued boots and an officer's hat. A long saber hung from his belt, and four flintlock pistols protruded from his belt; a long rifle was sheathed beside his saddle.

His long blond hair hung to his empty, pinned sleeve, and his blue eyes flashed like polar ice. Will rubbed the stubble of the yellowish beard that populated his face. He brushed his blonde mustache with his knuckles and flashed a mouth full of white teeth when he smiled. At such a sight, any man would be moved. The beauty was breathtaking.

Captain Forrester hadn't seen another living being in ten days, and that was the first sign of buffalo hunters in the distance. That was four days after he left the compound with Rusty Steel and Angus McFarlin. Levi Johnson was spending some time with Dahteste and her family in the Crow stronghold near the cabins. She wanted him to improve his Crow, and all Levi wanted was for her to learn English. He would have to wait until they returned to the compound; then, with Rusty, Angus, Dennis, and the boys, she would have to learn if she didn't want to be left out of their conversations.

When Will saw the buffalo hunters through his spyglass, he thought making contact wouldn't be wise. Most of the men you encountered in the Rocky Mountains were dangerous; many were hostile Indians. Will just wanted to ride on his own for a few weeks to try to figure out where he was headed. It appeared to have worked for Rusty Steel.

After spending the winter in the mountains alone, Rusty had even returned with a new friend, Dog. Forrester's expected future had seemed to vanish like a breath on a cold day. Now, he didn't know if he wanted to stay in the cabins in the compound or head farther west like he had initially planned. He still had an inkling to see California.

Will felt like a rudderless sailboat in calm waters, waiting for the wind to blow him wherever it wished. He was at the mercy of Mother Nature, like always in the Rockies. As he looked around, he felt the loneliness, but something else was in there too. He wasn't sure what it was, but he had a hint it was self-pity—something he despised.

Forrester wondered if there was a woman in his future like with his friend Levi. It had changed Johnson's life from one day to the next. Then again, he didn't know if that was what he wanted or not. Levi, indeed, hadn't expected it, but he appeared to be happy. Will didn't see himself marrying an Indian after being an Army captain. Levi's wife was almost as dangerous as Johnson. If the captain were to follow his friend's example, he might wake up one night with his throat cut. He just couldn't see it happening after what he had seen and done.

His best friend had just gotten married to a Crow war chief. Before that, they'd been at each other's side every day as they learned all there was to know about being mountain men, mainly learning how to survive.

They had both been taken on by Rusty Steel as apprentices. Actually, it was Levi that Rusty was impressed by. The captain was just lucky to be able to tag along.

He and Johnson were fast friends and companions. Levi was a quick study, but even Will had managed to learn what it took to live in such a harsh environment. He, too, could proudly call himself a mountain man— but was that what he wanted? Sometimes, his past still haunted him.

Will couldn't help but feel overwhelmed by all that had happened over the last year. His direction in life had changed with each situation, and now he was more puzzled than ever. Again, change was in the air, but he wasn't quite sure exactly what that change was. He felt he must tread with caution although he felt like running with abandon.

He clicked his tongue as they left the valley and began to climb a steep trail. He touched Blaze's flanks with his Army-issue spurs. The powerful animal responded. Two mountains created a gash of a gorge with nearly vertical cliffs. Some unknown ancient American Indian tribe had cut the trail out of the rock a millennium ago. It was only wide enough for a single horse to pass. On one side was a sheer cliff that climbed a hundred feet, and on the other was a drop-off into the abyss hundreds of feet below.

The West Point-educated ex-captain wasn't worried. His horse was used to the mountains after a long winter and was always surefooted. Blaze had carried him into war with the hostile Indians, and he made a handsome figure even if the Comanche did get the best of him and wipe out his expedition.

Every time he thought about it, his soul hurt. It was

eating away at his stomach like little rats. Expectation was man's worst enemy, so he tried to push all those busy thoughts from his head to focus on what he was doing and not feel sorry for himself.

In just over a year, Will had graduated from West Point, been commissioned to captain, and been given his first patrol. Levi Johnson worked with him as a scout once he hit the frontier forts in Kansas. He and his patrols had made frequent strikes against hostile Indians. Eventually, Forrester was honored by being given a history-breaking expedition. It was to find new locations to place more frontier forts farther west and deeper into the wilderness. He was to use his skills at mapmaking as he had learned back in New York.

The six-foot ex-soldier was very intelligent in military terms, and it was visible in his eyes. Forrester had also mastered the wilderness. Perhaps not as much as the natural, one-of-a-kind Levi Johnson, but he could hold his own. In a skirmish, he was a terror even with his missing arm. He had been named Blade due to his ferocity after besting the Sioux warrior in the Rendezvous.

That had been nearly a year ago. Now, he was twenty-eight years old and, at such a young age, had already left the Army to avoid disgrace. His last patrol had set out from Fort Scott, Kansas, just a little way from Fort Leavenworth. His name was changed again to Plainsman Bill and then to Plain Bill by Rusty Steel. At the end of the day, Captain was the only name that stuck. Some things, even the wilderness couldn't change.

That was when disaster struck. The Comanche made a final attack and nearly wiped out his entire expedition. Unfortunately, all the important members, including a famed professor, died in the onslaught of hostile warriors. Lucky for them, Will and Levi escaped alive.

The snow had melted on the trail, but now it was slippery with slush and mud. Steel shoes shot sparks as they clicked against the stone. Forrester pulled his horse to a stop and patted its neck.

"You're doing fine, boy," he said soothingly. "You can do this without me getting down, can't you? I trust your footing more than mine."

The stallion shook its mane and blew; then, it began to carefully make its way up the treacherous trail again. The captain pulled off his hat, which was slapped up on the side like the Seventh Calvary. He wiped his brow with his sleeve and replaced his cover. Beads of sweat glistened on his face and on the stallion's neck. The horse's tail swished, and his ears twitched as flies tried to alight on his eyes. He blew again, then got his footing and climbed farther. Blaze's horseshoes sounded loud against the stone ledge, but they were almost there.

Forrester's ears perked up. He could hear the roar of buffalo bulls in the distance. The sound was unmistakable. There must be bison in the next valley. He stood in his stirrups to get a better look. He still couldn't see the animals, but he saw the perpetual cloud of dust that hovered just over the herd. It smelled like buffalo, even from the other side of the mountain.

Now he saw why the Indians had gone to the effort of making such a stone trail. It was to get to the next valley, which seemed plentiful with wild game. Wildlife seemed abundant all around him. This was where they would travel yearly to find skins for their homes, food for their people, and tools from the bones; they even made sewing needles. No part of the bison was wasted. The captain had seen Indian children in the buffalo-killing fields happily feeding on sweetbreads as the parents worked.

The ex-Army officer clicked his tongue and gigged the stallion's flanks, and they shot for the top, which was now only thirty yards away. Will glanced down as a loose stone went sailing off the ledge and into the air and dropped into what appeared to be a green abyss: he couldn't see the bottom. He smiled as he thought back. Acrophobia had never been one of his weaknesses, but he'd had a roommate at West Point who was afraid of anything over shoulder high. Will never understood it.

Forrester suspected that even riding a horse made the man a little nervous because of the height. The odd thing about the officer was that when his feet were planted firmly on the ground, he was one of the bravest men Will had ever known. It was strange what the mind could do to the grittiest of men. Most men had a loud bark but didn't have the bite to back it up. He found it was the quiet ones that were truly dangerous.

The stallion stopped, but Will let it move along at his own pace. He was in no hurry. As the horse got its wind, the captain turned his face to the sun as the bright rays warmed his cheeks, making him smile. He might not know what direction to go in the future, but he knew he was in an incredibly beautiful place right now, and he took his time enjoying it.

In minutes, he would feast his eyes on vast numbers of buffalo. He might even have a run with the herd. He knew to stay clear and not mix in with the mass of animals. Sometimes, the slightest noise was enough to set them into a stampede. Then, everybody in the valley was in danger.

Will touched Blaze's flanks, but he didn't budge. Instead, the horse surprised the captain when it balked and tried to back down the trail. He had never shied away from a climb before and had seen herds of buffalo, so he wasn't afraid of what he smelled but still couldn't see.

"What's the matter?" Forrester asked while his horse got his footing. "We're almost there, big fella. You can do it."

The captain didn't dare dismount right then. His stallion seemed indecisive, which was a first. He was a war horse, used to all types of racket and dangerous situations, and he usually trusted his rider without question. Today, though, he wasn't in agreement with where they were heading.

"What in the world has got into you, Blaze?"

Suddenly, the stallion reared without warning, kicking its feet in the air. The first diamondback rattlesnake struck from a hidden crack in the cliff then was followed by a second, a third, and a fourth. Suddenly, a nest of a dozen snakes slithered across the narrow stone trail and sank their fangs into Blaze's front and back legs. The horse's eyes popped wide as he screamed and reared again, kicking his feet frantically. Will grabbed the saddle horn and leaned forward, nearly standing in his spurs to keep from being thrown off and into the void.

This time, snakes dangled from Blaze's limbs like some Biblical demon. Below them was a bottomless pit. It seemed to be calling out to Forrester. He tried to hold his balance but saw they would go down together if he stayed with his horse. Still, he wasn't sure he could jump clear and not fall over the edge. It was just over four feet wide.

The captain tried to step down, but Blaze reared again. This time, his steel shoes slipped, his legs went out from under him, and he rolled onto his back with Forrester underneath. The animal's weight slammed the captain onto the stone floor, banging his head on the side of the cliff on the way down. He was instantly dazed, and his lights went out.

The massive stallion tried to scramble to his feet, but it was too late, and he tumbled into the air, disappearing into the foliage somewhere below. He appeared to fall in slow motion as he kicked his feet. Snake's fangs still held his legs in their grasp as they all floated through the air, disappearing out of sight. The unconscious man didn't hear him breaking through the foliage as he crashed downward. Captain William Forrester lay unconscious on the stone trail. Blood pooled under his head. His breaths came in clamoring shudders, but he wasn't dead—at least not yet.

MEMORIES

A DOZEN VULTURES SAT ALONG THE NARROW TRAIL ABOVE and below the body, flapping their wings and squawking. As they edged nearer, they weren't sure if it was safe to take their first bite. A narrow stream of blood ran down his face from his head and disappeared under his shirt, pooling under his body. His neck looked twisted. Still, the predators sensed he was alive. Crows proved to be the bravest as they swooped perilously close to the downed rider, trying to snatch a bit of flesh in midflight.

The man groaned, and the buzzards startled and flapped their massive wings, whooshing as they hovered in midair over the drop-off, but they held their ground. This wouldn't be the first animal they ate while it was still alive. It didn't matter to them whether he was breathing or not. It would be fresh meat for those who usually ate the dead. Even a vulture liked a warm kill. Soon, other scavengers would appear, and the battle would ensue for the human remains. Turkey vultures, ravens, crows, coyotes, and even raccoons would fight for the right to feed on the dead man.

The captain's pupils jerked under his eyelids. His eyelashes fluttered as he tried to force himself to come around. He groaned again and opened his mouth. Blood poured out. He moved his tongue around his cheeks and spat out a molar. He blinked, but everything was blurry. He pulled his arm from under his body. A flintlock pistol was in his fist.

A hammer clicked, and a gunshot rang out. A hovering buzzard exploded in a puff of blood and feathers, then dropped out of sight. Gun smoke curled from the barrel. The others flapped their wings and used the thermal currents to escape, finally circling above, chattering among themselves. They were patient and would hover over the body all day if need be. For the vultures, it was an effortless glide on hot air. Soon, other scavengers would arrive too. They felt sure the human wouldn't survive, and it was just a matter of time. They patiently waited with hungry eyes, all squawking in the distance.

The captain gritted his teeth and pushed himself up to sit as he leaned his back against the cliff wall. His head spun for a moment, but it slowly stopped. The officer's heart hammered between his temples as his head throbbed in pain, and his neck hurt. White bone glared in the sunlight from a gash in his skull. The soldier laid the gun on the ground and raised his hand to feel his wound. He winced as his fingertips touched bone.

He flipped the flap of skin back over the wound and pressed it into place, hair and all. The soldier got light-headed, then dizzy, and once again, his eyes crawled back into his head. He let out a long chattering breath. It sounded like his last, but he finally inhaled again. He was still alive, at least for now.

A vulture was pecking at his leather boots when he came around again. He opened his eyes, and the bird turned its head to the side, staring back with one eye. It clucked as it drew back to peck again. The captain pulled a second gun. Another bird exploded and was knocked off its feet. It was shot from such a point-blank range, its feathers caught fire. It tumbled down the trail and disappeared over the edge. As the captain's head cleared, he looked around but didn't know where he was. Confusion filled his eyes as he tried to calm down and slow his breathing. He coughed, and bolts of electricity shot through his ribs. His body was broken, but he wasn't dead. The pain proved it.

There seemed to be too much blood on the trail to be just his. He crawled on hands and knees to the cliff's edge and peered down but couldn't see anything below except green. It appeared to be impossible to see the bottom. The man in a buckskin shirt and pants wondered where he was as he looked up at the sheer cliff. Then it hit him.

In his mind's eye, faces passed at the speed of light like they were on a tumbler, but he didn't seem to know who they were. He closed his eyes and shook his head, but still, he couldn't see past the cobwebs. The cavalryman heard buffalo roar in the next valley. He knew instantly what it was. Was he after the bison when he was injured? He heard shots from heavy-caliber long guns.

He looked up and down the steep trail and wondered where he had come from, the top or the bottom. The chiseled stone path was an industrial undertaking and looked as ancient as the mountains. That didn't tell him where he was but just made things seem more surreal. Maybe he had died, and he just didn't know it yet.

He looked at the sky and whispered in a rusty voice, "Keep with me, Lord. We can get through this."

His brain raced and spun out of control, and he reeled and nearly lost consciousness again. Not only couldn't he remember where he was, he couldn't remember *who* he was either. The captain began to hyperventilate, and his head twirled around and around. He didn't remember yesterday or even what happened today.

He looked down at his clothes and instinctively knew he was an officer. He saw the hat on the ground and the silver spurs on his boots. The saber on his belt said he was a captain, but why was he wearing Indian clothing? There were too many questions and no answers.

That was when he saw hoofprints in the slosh a few yards down the trail. The captain pushed himself to his feet and used the cliff wall to steady himself as he walked ten feet to the prints. They were large, and the horse was shoed. He peered over the edge and to the deep drop-off, but there was no sign of a horse. All he saw was a thick stand of trees more than three hundred feet below.

It seemed even farther. As the captain stared into the void, he became dizzy again and felt like it was calling him to let himself go and end it all. It would be so easy to succumb to the easy way out. But the captain hadn't sought to take the easy way out his entire life. He'd chosen high ground, and if there were challenges, all the better.

"If I did have a horse, I sure as hell don't now," the captain said. "Nothing could have survived that fall."

He deduced the animal was spooked and fell off the cliff. Still, he couldn't see *why* that happened. He was lucky not to go over with the horse, but still, he was injured and worse for wear. There wasn't anywhere on his body that didn't produce agony. He could walk, but each step sent bolts of pain through his body. He was a mass of cuts and bruises and had a sizable hole in his head. He was suffering from a concussion.

The captain dropped to one knee to catch his breath and pulled off his bandana. He wrapped it over his head and tied it under his chin to keep the skin of his cracked skull from flopping out of place. He wobbled as he tried to stay upright.

He pushed his yellow hair out of his face and looked at the sun. It was overhead. Then he heard the buffalo over the summit and pushed himself to his feet again but had to lean against the rock wall to keep from falling. He looked at the trail of blood he left where he fell. Rifle shots cracked again in the distance.

The side of his neck and shirt were stained red. The captain still didn't have any idea of what happened. Maybe he was attacked by wild Indians. Or even bandits, although he had no clue at all, not even a hint; he saw no arrows nor footprints. All he saw were the tracks of what he'd deduced was his horse.

The officer looked around on the ground for his hat. It was an Army captain's. Then he looked at his feet and saw Army-issue officers' boots. A shiny saber hung from his belt, and fancy silver spurs jangled on his heels. The rest of him was torn and bloody. He took the time to reload the two spent pistols and check the prime on the other two.

He wondered if he had a rifle, too, down there at the bottom of the abyss, wherever it was. If he did, it probably hadn't survived the fall. His four small guns would have to do. At least he had a powder horn full of gunpowder and a pouch full of caps and balls. He looked across the void to the mountain on the other side. It, too, was covered densely in trees.

The captain looked down the trail and then up. Going down would be more accessible, and down the mountains would be more desirable than up, but something in him said no. He was to climb. For some reason, he felt that was the direction he'd been going in before whatever happened, happened.

He couldn't say why, but it mattered little. Despite the mysterious situation, the captain felt calm and in control. Even if his deduction was correct and he'd lost his memory in the fall, he instinctively knew he had to control his feelings and show no fear. He was an Army captain, after all.

Once the initial shock passed, he knew what had happened. He felt he was a studied scholar and knew what amnesia was. That was what he was suffering from. He felt his head again and knew that was how it happened. He didn't know why he should go up rather than down—he just knew.

The twenty steps to the summit seemed eternal as the captain dragged one foot in front of the other. He had to stop every two or three steps to catch his breath. It was jagged, short, and fast. It felt like it took an hour to walk twenty yards. Maybe it did: he could barely stand. Finally, his eyes reached the top, and he gazed at a green valley. In the center stood a lone buffalo. Hundreds of head lay dead on the ground, ready to be skinned.

A two-wheel cart pulled by a horse transported the valuable tongues and hides out of the valley. He could hear millions of flies in the distance, and the stench reached him like a punch to the stomach. He was gazing at the killing fields. Bloody red carcasses of skinned bison covered the valley floor.

The captain watched as the only standing buffalo's front knees buckled, and it dropped to the ground. Then came the report of the gunshot. He turned toward the sound and saw three buffalo hunters standing on a massive flat rock just over the valley. Three tripods stood before them, holding up the heavy hexagonal barrels of their rifles.

The captain immediately knew the sound. He must have had a similar gun himself. Maybe it, too, went down with his horse. But why? What could have happened? He felt he was knowledgeable in the wilderness and wasn't afraid now that he knew what was happening. He would have to take a chance and talk to the buffalo hunters. He tapped his finger on his pistol grip. He didn't even notice. It was like a nervous tic.

The captain didn't even consider what was being done or the consequences. He wasn't aware of anything other than his brain. It seemed to work fine except for his memory. He looked down questioningly at his missing arm. He hadn't even noticed. It was like it was always that way. He wondered if he had lost it in battle. He sighed and sat on an old, lightning-racked tree stump overlooking the massacre. Another strange tree stood over him. It was shaped like an aging mother. It looked like the tree was praying over a grave.

The captain pushed himself up, forced the pain out of his mind, and moved as quickly as his broken body would take him. He didn't think he had to hurry, though. There was still a lot of work to do, skinning the dead buffalo scattered from one end of the valley to the other. He hardly noticed. He didn't have enough personal information to react to anything. He was steeling himself up to accept losing his memory. Now, he had to make sure he didn't lose his life too.

In the distance, he saw the three shooters climb down from the rock and disappear, only to reappear again a few minutes later as they rode their horses into the valley floor.

CROW INDIANS

DAHTESTE OPENED HER EYES, YAWNED, AND STRETCHED her arms over her head. She laid her hand beside her and felt for Levi, but he wasn't there. Her smile turned into a frown, then a look of curiosity. It was early, so the spring air was cool. Dying embers made her face glow orange as she stood, wrapped herself, and moved for the tipi flap.

"Levi," Dahteste called in Crow. "Are you outside?" But still no answer.

She pulled her thick grizzly bear robe tight and stepped barefoot out of the tipi. The sun shone on her olive-skinned face and danced in her eyes. Her husband had just finished packing the mule with supplies. Saddled horses stood behind the beast of burden as they shifted their feet, eager to go.

"Are you going somewhere?" Dahteste asked as surprise crossed her face. Then she frowned. "Are you leaving me?"

"No, *we're* going somewhere," Levi said in English,

laughing. "We're gonna go down and visit my old pards. I've already made up breakfast, so grab yourself somethin' to eat before we set off. The mule and horses can wait for ya, darlin'."

Dahteste stood at the door of the tipi with a puzzled look. She blinked her big brown eyes, but Levi just laughed some more. His eyes were full of mischief and shined when he looked at his Crow wife. She'd thought she had him completely under her spell, but she had mistakenly assumed her husband had the ways of one of her warriors. He had outsmarted her.

"We've put it off long enough, Dahteste," Levi said. "Now it's time for you to learn English."

"But we just got here!" she protested. "I haven't said goodbye to my family."

"I did it for you." Levi laughed. "Oh, I know you're a war chief and all, but I'm your husband, and I've got a say-so in things too. We've been here in the Crow stronghold layin' around, gettin' fat, so it's time to go and check on our second home. Remember, we've got another tipi back in the compound. Or have ya already forgotten about it? Maybe we can even bag an elk on the way. Today, we might just get lucky."

"We should talk to Chief Hachta before we leave. He might not like us running off," Dahteste said. She almost stuttered as she felt things getting out of her control. "He might have something important for me to do. Remember, I'm a war chief."

"Nope, there ain't a thing he had for ya to do, 'cause I've already checked." Levi laughed. "As a matter of fact, he seemed pretty happy to get rid of ya."

"Chief Hachta said that? No, he didn't. You're

making that up. You've tricked me." She forced a frown, but her eyes were laughing too.

"Come on, darlin', we're burnin' daylight," Levi said, grinning like a possum. "Stuff those biscuits with bacon and bring 'em with us. We can eat 'em while we ride. There's fresh coffee over there to wake you up."

Her bare feet pushed tiny dust clouds as she walked to the fire and filled a tin cup with coffee. Vapor rose from the kettle in the early morning air, which was filled with the aroma of freshly perked java.

The Plains Indians were nomads by nature, so once Dahteste got the plan clear in her head, it took her no time to put her personal travel kit together. After three cups of coffee each, they mounted up and walked their horses toward the end of the camp and the single trail to the compound and the three cabins. Levi had bathed in the Crow culture for the last eight weeks, and although he enjoyed it, he longed for some time with his friends, talking on Angus and Rusty's porch—and in his own language.

Like everything else Levi did, he did it with apparent ease. He was sharp as a tack and a very quick study. With the Crow words he already knew and what he had learned living with an Indian woman, his vocabulary was large, and he understood how to speak honorably to his brothers and sisters of the tribe. When he was in the camp, he was one of them, and they treated him accordingly. That was something he hadn't expected at all.

He had believed there would be too much jealousy for him to be welcomed by everybody for at least a year, if ever. But that had not turned out to be the case. The Crow people in the area knew him better than he had ever imagined. The chief knew that Levi's trapping, tracking, and hunting skills were second to none, not even the chief's.

Chief Hachta was a clever man, and as soon as Levi was a week in camp and had consummated his wedding, he began to pick his brain for all his beaver-trapping skills. Cold-water pelts were the only way he could get more rifles from the White men. Maybe this season, he would be allowed to buy two with the help of Levi Beaver Johnson. The mountain men were cautious about how many long rifles they sold to the different tribes. They didn't want those very barrels turned on them one day in the future.

This had been Rusty's policy for years, and it had kept them out of trouble and, at the same time, provided some weapons to his Indian friends. They needed guns to hunt more game to feed the growing tribe. There was also the threat of the Army. If they thought the Crow were arming themselves, they might act against them as a precautionary measure. It was better not to make too much noise and keep the Army far from the camp.

Of course, the Indians immediately called Levi Beaver. The American Indians gave special members of their tribes unique names describing the person; they could even have two or three in a lifetime, depending on how their life developed for better or worse.

His wife's name was Dahteste, which meant Warrior Woman. The name was given to her by Chief Hachta. Some names came with great respect, and others came with shame and ridicule. If you acted like some animal in the forest, you would be given this animal's name. The language was Absaroka from the Siouan linguistic stock. Long ago, they were related to the Hidatsa of the upper Missouri River.

Of course, Levi also looked forward to seeing his best buddy again, Captain Will Forrester. They had come west together, for better and often for worse. It had been a long time, considering they hadn't split up since they'd partnered up back in Kansas. Even though it had only been just over a year, it seemed like a lifetime ago to both men.

He knew it must have been a shock for the captain. It had even been a shock for Levi. Before he met his Crow war chief, the last thing on his mind was marriage, especially to a fierce Indian woman. She had proved to have a mind of her own too. He had never met any woman like her. There was a perpetual burning fire in her eyes.

Beaver had thought he had too much to do before he settled down and had a family. As strange as it seemed, that was precisely what he felt like now that he had his wife. He briefly wondered how that would work out with a war chief. He was tied to the Crow tribe even more than Rusty Steel, who was the blood brother of the chief. Still, marrying into the tribe and winning their blessing was a great mountain to scale. But he not only had the tribe's benediction, he also had their admiration. He was a skilled mountain man and had captured the heart of the woman all the warrior braves had dreamed of marrying.

Levi had already made a reputation among the Indians who frequented the Rocky Mountains. It was like he stepped into a whirlwind, and Dahteste was thrown in with him, and they were spat out together. He still couldn't fit all the pieces together to describe his feelings and precisely what and how it happened. It was one of those mysteries of life. Nobody had the answer to it. His skills had been observed from afar, and most Crow scouts said his hunting and trapping were the best of any man they had seen—even the Indians themselves. Like Angus always said, Levi was one-of-a-kind.

As they rode down the first narrow trail and into the forest, rays of sun slanted through the leaves like rain. The trees were alive with the noisy chatter of a dozen species of birds. The horses' hooves were silent on the soft earth. Only the occasional nicker or whinny gave them away, but they weren't expecting complications between the Crow camp and the compound. It was only a few hours away, and Chief Hachta's people would be everywhere, even though they wouldn't see them.

Dahteste would occasionally point out a feather or a bow sticking out above the tall grass. She often did the spying, so she knew all the best hiding spots. Only when Levi lived in the camp did he understand how much they policed the mountains and their territory. They knew when a mountain lion stepped foot onto their land. Such awareness made them invincible high in the Rocky Mountains.

If the US Army had to go up there to get them and force them to reservations, they would lose half their men the first month. Surviving year-round was as harsh an environment as any of them knew. But the Crow had been there for many years, and they knew everything there was to know about the mountains. They were the masters of survival in these peaks, valleys, and canyons.

"It's high time you learned some decent English," Levi said. "Whatcha gonna do come Rendezvous time? You know we plan to spend the whole two weeks there.

It'll be the first time I've seen other folks for a whole year. I reckon by the time you can understand Angus and Rusty, you'll be ready." He reached across and stroked her face with the back of his hand.

"You know Chief Hachta doesn't like his warriors to visit the Rendezvous," Dahteste huffed and furrowed her brow. She batted her eyelashes at Johnson but to no avail. The foggy spell he had been lost in for the last two months was finally clearing, and he was itching to get back to his old habits.

Beaver just laughed. He had already learned all her tricks to get him to do what she wanted. He was surprised that Indian women were just like white and black women. They were all bossy as the dickens.

"That's because they get so drunk, they give away their pelts. Hard liquor don't settle well with Indian folks. So, ya see? You've got nothin' to worry about. I never drink too much, and you don't drink at all. As far as the pelts go, I've already talked to the chief, and I'm gonna sell the tribe's furs this year. I'll get twice the price that a Crow Indian would. I know it ain't fair, but it is what it is. So, you'll be there in the name of your people. You don't wanna let 'em down, do ya?"

Levi grinned like a possum. He had planned and schemed to figure out how to take his wife to see his friends and then to the meeting. He knew if he waited until after the Rendezvous, he would miss out on the only attraction they had in the Rocky Mountains, and the longer he waited, the harder it would be to get Dahteste to go. It was the yearly fur trading company meeting, with free liquor and loads of competitions with prizes. They would all go together to the Rendezvous. He imagined himself and Dahteste together. It was going to come as a surprise to more than a few.

"I don't know if I trust being in a place with White men all around me," Dahteste said. "It sounds dangerous to me. If they touch me, I will cut their tongues out."

"How do you know it's so dangerous if you ain't ever been there? And nobody is gonna cut anybody's tongue out." Levi laughed. "Like most folks, you're just scared of what you don't know. It's called the fear of the unknown, darlin'."

The trail widened, and they rode stirrup-to-stirrup, with the mule trailing. Levi beamed as he unveiled his plan. He knew that if he had talked to Dahteste first, it would have been more complicated. But the chief understood that she was Levi's woman now, and even a war chief had to do her duties as a wife, just like Levi did as a husband. When Johnson offered to sell the tribe's cold-water beaver pelts for top dollar, it sealed the deal; Dahteste couldn't say no even if she wanted to.

"I hope the bears haven't been in our tipi," Dahteste said.

"Angus and Rusty are keepin' an eye on it for us. The captain said he was gonna ride off for a spell just like Rusty did. I reckon us two hookin' up and getting hitched must have come as a surprise to 'im. I know it did to me." Levi laughed.

Halfway to the compound, they got lucky, and Levi saw an elk. It was a nice twelve-pointer known as a six-by-six to the mountain men. It stood on a hill downwind on the other side of a small gorge. Dahteste kicked her foot over her pony's neck and silently dropped to the ground. She pulled her bow from her shoulder and strung an arrow. She looked up just when Beaver was taking his shot. It was a perfect hit, and the big buck dropped like a sack of potatoes.

"It looks like we're gonna be lucky on this trip." Levi grinned. "It's about time we had a little good luck. Now we've got some elk meat to celebrate with. They'll have a little corn liquor for my coffee too."

THREE CABINS

"DAGNABIT, WHERE'D YA HIDE THE JUG OF CORN LIQUOR?"
Rusty grumbled as soon as he got up and stepped onto
the porch. "How am I supposed to have a coffee without
a splash to give it some kick? Go on and tell me where
you hid it. You know it belongs here in the center of the
table. Why do ya keep movin' it on me, you old fool?"

"You're the old fool!" Angus spat. "You've got the
brain of an ant."

"I didn't quite catch that," Rusty growled as he
wiggled his finger in his ear. "Say it again 'cause I don't
think I like what cha said."

"Leave it be, pilgrim," Angus said. "You don't need to
keep sawin' on it. I'll get the jug. It's just I think we've
been havin' a nip too early of a day, it bein' breakfast
and all. That's why we ain't getting nothin' done. That,
and the fact that you don't like to help. You are about as
valuable as a dirt clod."

"Like I've been sayin' to anyone who'll listen, I
always do my share of the chores," Rusty laughed. "It's

just, you take work to a whole other level. A man don't have to start an hour before daylight and not stop until an hour after dark. The Lord knows you hardly sleep. I've never seen a man who likes to work more than relax. Ain't that right, Dog?"

The massive canine lay on Rusty's feet. Every time Angus grumbled at his master, Dog barred his teeth, but Angus had already made friends and knew he was just becoming like his owner—ornery and cantankerous. The dog didn't even bother to lift its head. It was used to the mornings with the two bickering mountain men. After a couple of coffees, Rusty simmered down, and Angus saw it like he did every day. Trying to get Rusty to work more than he did was an impossible task.

Still, every morning, the two argued about who did more chores. Or it was more like a daily reminder of Rusty's position on hard work. Just because he was lazy at home didn't mean he was lazy when things went sideways, hunting or trapping. He had proven himself to one and all. He was one of the most dangerous men on the mountain, and he had shown it often enough to have a reputation all the way to the Montana Plains.

"Heck, it ain't no secret you do more than I do." Rusty cackled. "Everybody knows that. You do more than everybody, even the mules. You'd think you'd know better at your age. You should be ashamed of yourself. You'd think a man would slow down after a couple of decades of livin' in the wilderness. You've got to learn how to calm down and enjoy life. Stop to smell the roses before it's too late. Now, I know how to take my time and do my chores and still have time for a nap and a drink."

"I guess one man's meat is another man's poison,"

Angus said, bunching his lips into a pout. "But a rollin' stone don't gather no moss."

"I must admit no moss is gonna collect on you." Rusty grinned and said, "But, ya see, one man's gain ain't necessarily another man's loss."

"Of late, your idea of a good time is sittin' here watching your dog bark." Angus snickered. "I still can't get used to callin' 'im by such a stupid name. Who in the world calls their mutt Dog?"

"Me, that's who." Rusty grinned, as stubborn as an overloaded, three-legged mule. "Like I told ya, he's my dog, and I'll call 'im any danged thing I wanna."

Angus finally shrugged, making his face look like a shriveled old orange. He knew he worked too much, but that's how he had always been. And ever since Rusty Steel arrived in the compound, he had done his share but not a grain more. It wasn't so much that he didn't like to work. What it was, he liked to sit and think over a good pipe of tobacco; you couldn't do both simultaneously.

McFarlin's problem was he didn't know how to relax even though he was getting on in years. Maybe he couldn't wade waist-deep in the freezing streams anymore, but he did more work than anybody except Levi Johnson. Then again, he wasn't living with them anymore. Levi chopped wood for the entire compound. It was enough to last all winter, and he did it in a few days. Angus admired a man with his work ethic. Sometimes he wondered why he and Rusty were such good friends. They were as different as night and day.

The tipi stood between Mountain Dennis's cabin and theirs. Rusty could see that Angus had already been up and had opened the flap to air it out. It wouldn't do to get the damp spring air inside, or it could ruin the furs. It was still piled deep in buffalo and bear skins. Sometimes, Rusty snuck inside, all alone, remembering his adventures as he puffed on his ceramic bowl and his eyes reflected orange in the embers.

Mountain Dennis strolled over from his cabin with a knife and a piece of wood in his hand. He was so used to the two bickering he hardly heard what they said.

"Here comes another lazy one," Angus growled. "I don't know which of you two is worse."

"Whatcha doin', Dennis?" Rusty asked, ignoring what his roommate said.

"Whittlin' and a-rockin'," he said as he sat on the porch glider with a piece of pine wood in one hand and a pocketknife in the other.

"Whittlin'?" Angus asked, frowning. "Don't you have enough work to do without sittin' around carvin' out critters?"

"What ya makin' now, Dennis?" Rusty smiled.

"Yep, whittlin'." Dennis smiled. "I've taken up a new hobby. All ya do is take a lump of wood, and if you sit long enough, something's bound to happen. Anybody knows that iffin you ever owned a chicken. Why, I don't rightly know what it'll be, Rusty. It might be a rooster or maybe a duck. I already whittled me a horse. Once ya start, it goes faster than weeds in skunk grass."

Angus sniffed the air first, then Dennis, who had the sharpest nose. Their smiles dropped from their faces. Rusty smelled it too. Horses were coming. Distant hoof steps neared the trail to the Crow camp. The mountain man didn't expect Levi to show up for a few months, if at all that summer. They had seen the look in his eyes when he was with Dahteste and knew he was hooked like a beached trout. Usually, if somebody came unannounced, it was bad news, so they each laid a brace of pistols on the table beside their tin cups of whiskey-laced coffee.

"Who in the world could it be now?" Rusty huffed. "We've had too much contact with the Crow tribe of late, and that ain't good even if they are our friends. I figure iffin they see White men too often, they'll begin to feel they're being pushed out."

"But you're Chief Hachta's blood brother," Dennis replied. "It can't be nothin' that bad, even if it is the chief."

"Usually, when the chief plans to come or have his warriors bring a message, someone sends up smoke signals first to avoid misunderstandings and surprises, which could lead to violence. There ain't been but a couple of wispy clouds in the sky for the last week. It ain't like the Crow to show up unannounced."

Rusty clicked his tongue and spat a stream of brown juice off the side of the porch, then wiped his mouth with his sleeve. His long hair and beard made him look like a woolly bear in his buckskins.

"Well, if we can already smell the horses, it won't be but a half hour before they're here," Angus whispered. "It used to be I could smell a man an hour away, but I reckon I'm getting old, and the old sniffer don't work as well as it used to. I don't like unexpected company, even if it is springtime. Strangers are rarely welcome up here on the mountain."

They heard the clopping of walking horses get nearer. The sound echoed through the forest. There was clearly more than one animal. Angus tilted his head, focused on the sound, and showed Rusty and Dennis three fingers. Then he snatched a pistol up in each hand, as did the other two. Hammers clacked as they waited, and eyes narrowed. There was hardly a breath of air. A wasp hovered over the open jug, and Rusty swatted it away.

"Pesky buggers," Steel spat. The wasp tumbled through the air, then launched again and flew to the mud nest on the back of the compound fence. A dozen insects circled their home, ready to fend off aggressors. Every living thing in the mountains lived in perpetual danger, even the bugs.

The three men turned toward the north trail out of the compound. They could see it just beyond the zigzag fence. They waited with flintlock pistols in their white-knuckled fists as sweat glistened on their faces. They were all suddenly awake and sharp as needles. They didn't know what to expect when the riders wheeled around the corner.

Crows cawed in the trees. They were sending out the alarm that someone was coming. A dozen sat perched on a long, bare limb like pallbearers dressed in black. They protested the arrival of strangers. A horse neighed in the distance, and another answered. Movement could be seen through the trees. Whoever they were, they would show at any moment.

———

TWO HORSES LUMBERED down the trail with a mule following on a lead. Dahteste grabbed Levi's sleeve, and he pulled to a stop. He saw his feelings reflected in her expression. Hesitation and curiosity filled their eyes. He shrugged and smiled—it was clear that it was from his heart. Beaver drew an anxious breath and looked past Dahteste toward the bottom of the path.

They were just about to arrive at the compound. Another hour and they would be there. Levi knew this part of the mountain like the back of his hand. He also knew every nook and cranny where an enemy could hide. His wife's eyes flashed, looking for any signs of danger. The closer they came to the compound, the more nervous she got.

Emotion bombarded Johnson's brain as he felt torn between the Crow Indians' life he had recently accepted as his own and his home with other people of his kind —his only friends. He hoped things would go well between his buddies and his new wife. She was as proud a woman as he had ever met. He wondered if that was a good thing or a bad one. Time would tell if they fit in as a couple, or if Dahteste could be convinced to live there in the compound. At the moment, he had only said it was for a visit.

Angus and his wife moved from the cabins to the stronghold all year around. Often in the summer, she would disappear, and McFarlin would go to the Rendezvous. But come winter, Angus would head for Pine Needle's tipi, and he would let her feed him and keep him warm through the coldest months. Despite his age and scruffy appearance, he was famous for his dancing skills, and all the Crow women were after him. It was a phenomenon that even Rusty Steel didn't understand.

Of course, his wife wasn't a war chief, and the chief hardly paid her attention. He was always busy with the elders, medicine men, and warriors. They both liked things just like they were too. No one expected anything from them except for some beaver pelts, which Angus supplied every spring to keep the relationship beneficial to the tribe. It wouldn't be the same with Levi and Dahteste, though. She was an important war chief; now, he had become as famous a mountain man as Rusty Steel. It was still unclear what would be expected of Dahteste and Levi in the future.

Of course, they both wanted to be together, but they also wanted to stay with the people they were used to living with. Levi had enjoyed living with the Crow people, and they had made every effort to make him welcome despite the color of his skin. No one treated him like a White man. They treated him like he had always been there and was one of them. Nobody stared and pointed at his pale skin like at first. The chief had made it clear he was to be honored like another warrior. This was a big thing. Much bigger than Levi ever imagined. It, too, would come with its eventual obligations— something else Levi wasn't yet aware of.

The young hunters of the tribe came to Beaver with their fish traps, and he helped them modify them to make them better. The few with rifles asked him for tips while hunting elk. He was a good find for Chief Hachta, and they openly showed their appreciation too. He was invited to any important hunting party, and his wife always accompanied him.

When Levi looked at Dahteste, they didn't have to say anything. Their eyes pretty much said it all, locking on each other's faces, flickering in surprise, and then thought. A simple nod and smile were enough to say a hundred words. Levi had found the Crow people to be sensitive and very polite. It was frowned on to be a bully and punishable by the chief. All they wanted to do was continue to live like they had for a thousand years.

Now, the buffalo were nearly gone on the southern plains, and wild game was scarcer every year, even in the Rockies. Soon, they believed the buffalo would disappear from the northern plains near the mountains too. Then they would have to move or starve. The chief and a chosen few knew what awaited their tribe. Hachta tried every way he could to prolong the inevitable.

The chief kept the truth from his people for their own well-being. Rusty Steel was the only one who knew what was to come. It wouldn't be right then, but it wouldn't take forever. The civilization machine was pushing westward like a Baldwin locomotive, and it was unstoppable, and millions of immigrants were behind it. It was inevitable as the sun rising in the sky every morning.

"All right." He exhaled a breath and chuckled. "Are you ready? This'll be the last Crow I'm gonna speak to ya for the next week. It ain't like you don't know my friends. When I went to your camp, I only knew the chief, and that was just barely. When I was around him, he was always talkin' with Rusty. He'd hardly glanced at me."

"You can't do that!" Dahteste cried. "That's not fair. When we're alone, we must speak Crow!"

"No, ma'am, we mustn't." Levi laughed. "Now you're gonna start actin' like a normal wife and not a war chief. Maybe it'll do ya some good to simmer that temper of yours down a notch or two." He laughed some more. "That's the same thing you did to me. I ain't spoken a dozen words of English for two months. I've got words kickin' around in my brain that's bustin' to get out. I hope the boys are up to a good jaw waggin' 'cause I intend to bend their ears for hours. Come on now; I wanna surprise my friends. We're gonna be quiet as puppies walkin' on cotton so we surprise 'em when we arrive."

BUFFALO HUNTERS

THREE WOOLLY-LOOKING MEN RODE ACROSS THE VALLEY floor, each leading three mules piled high with buffalo skins. Thousands of flies buzzed around their heads as they lit on the bloody hides. The head of the group of hunters wore a rabbit fur hat, a light buckskin shirt, and britches. Several pistols stuck from his belt, and a rifle was sheathed on either side of his saddle.

The horses lazily clopped across soft ground. The riders would occasionally stop to rest. The horses and mules pulled at the odd tuft of grass and slid their jaws. Buffalo tracks were everywhere. Where there was once an ocean of tall grass blowing in waves now lay land barren to the nub. A massive herd of over fifty thousand head had passed across that very valley the day before. There were still fifty million buffalo on the plains.

The freckle-faced hunter followed the man on point. He was barrel-chested and broad-shouldered with curly red hair and a walrus mustache. He dozed and rocked in his saddle as the mules struggled under the load. Drool ran from his mouth and down his chin, but still, he didn't stir.

"Wake up, Bud," Virgil Lovejoy growled. "Keep your eyes open, moron. If the Indians catch you asleep, they'll take your scalp before you've time to open your eyes."

Bud Guns rubbed his eyes with his fists and yawned. He waved his hand before his face to shoo the flies away. Behind him rode a third rider, and behind him, three more mules. They could barely bear the weight of the heavy skins. The man riding drag kept looking behind him. Paranoia sat perched on his shoulder.

"It'd be just like the Indians to let us do all the work, then they steal our hides and take our scalps too, so don't be sleepin' in your saddle, 'cause we need all the eyes on deck," Clinch West spat as he looked back yet again. "If you were in the Army, you'd be shot for sleepin' on the job."

"Well, I ain't in the Army, fool," Bud snarled. "And you ain't anymore either, so don't go bossin' me around."

While Bud was sassing back at Clinch, Virgil pulled to a stop, and when Bud's horse walked by, he dropped him. The backhand came so quickly that he didn't see it coming. He suddenly felt himself tumbling out of his saddle and into the dirt, as his brain spun out of control and stars danced around his head.

"Whatcha do that for?" Bud asked as he rubbed his jaw. A knot was forming on his forehead. "Black men ain't supposed to hit White men. They'd hang ya for that in some places back east. Don't forget who you are."

Virgil looked at the lowest man on the totem pole and sighed. "In the mountains, I'm just like you are, stupid. There ain't no color up here, exceptin' Indians.

For them, we all be trespassers. Remember who you're workin' for. I ain't no slave you can talk back to. If you don't like the way I run things, you can take your horse and ride on out of here, but you'll be goin' on your own. Otherwise, close your gob and open your eyes. Now get up out of the dirt. We're wastin' daylight."

The boss was tall and as solid as a rock. He was also the best shot of the hunting party of three. The only reason they had let Bud come along was because he knew how to shoot. He was the only other taker when Virgil decided to form a group of hunters to ride into the wilderness and make their fortune. With hides worth up to ten dollars a square foot, they would acquire a nice pouch of gold. The hides were worth so much due to their lack of smell, their durability, and their softness. A buffalo blanket could last a lifetime. Now, they had to do the tricky part: make it out of the Rocky Mountains alive with the skins intact.

"I'm gonna ride out front a mile or two to make sure nobody's waitin' out there to ambush us. There's more money on the back of them mules than I've ever seen in my life, so don't you dare fall asleep again, Bud. Do you hear me?"

Bud nodded but was still angry for getting back-handed and didn't want to reply.

"I didn't hear you, boy," Virgil growled. When his eyes locked with Bud's, the White man flinched. For a moment, he thought he saw tombstones instead of pupils.

"I hear ya, boss," Bud replied as he stared at his boots. "I won't fall asleep no more."

Without another word, the hunting party leader took off at a trot as he rode down the mountain until his image disappeared over a rise. As soon as he saw Virgil vanish, Clinch became even more nervous. He knew how skilled Lovejoy was, and although he felt up to the chore, he doubted that Bud would be if he were pressed into a bad situation. He preferred to have his old friend Virgil beside him rather than Mr. Guns. He knew the man was as lazy as the day was long, but they needed the extra gun. Especially now that they had the furs and had to get out of the mountains.

The head of the hunting party got as much distance from his smelly skins as possible to see if any surprises were in store for them. He knew that they would run into trouble before they got out of the mountains. He rode out of the forest and into a gorge with vertical cliffs. He remembered it from the trip to the hunting grounds. He was surprised his bearings were so spot-on. That was when he saw the White man.

Virgil drew in a deep breath; a dim pallor replaced his usual complexion. He stared, seemingly re-evaluating. He tapped his index finger on his pistol grip. The injured man hadn't seen him yet. He wondered what he was doing without a horse or mule in the middle of nowhere. Lovejoy wheeled his mount toward the White man with long blond hair. He smiled as he considered the contrast—one was as white as sugar and the other as brown as an oak. He wondered if he was another of those southern gentlemen who weren't genteel. It was apparent he was a soldier despite his buckskin garb.

The Black hunter dropped off his horse and grabbed the lead. His animal clopped across stone, making sparks fly. Virgil cleared his throat and kept his hand close to his pistol. Then he saw the saber and knew he was an officer. Now, he was too curious to let it be.

Lovejoy was a man of curious nature. That was what had brought him to the Rocky Mountains, like many. It would be impossible for him to ride on. Especially as the man appeared to be wounded, and despite Lovejoy's rugged appearance, he had a kind heart deep inside. He could not resist helping someone in need, even if he smelled trouble. From his experience, Black men and White authorities seldom got along, but just the same, the man was obviously wounded.

"Howdy there, pilgrim," Virgil said in a loud, clear voice. He kept his hand on his pistol grip just in case. But the man looked too dazed to present a problem. "Are you all right there, friend?"

The captain looked at the stranger and blinked. His voice surprised him and broke his trance. He was still suffering from the crushing blow but had no recollection of what had happened to him. Still, he felt like he had a half dozen broken ribs, and who knew what damage was inside. A rivulet of blood seeped from the edge of his mouth and down his chin.

"I'm afraid I'm a little worse for wear," the captain said. "I must have fallen and lost my horse over the cliff. There are hoofprints up there a way."

"Where you headed?" Virgil asked as he laid his hands on the pommel and leaned forward, more curious by the moment. "My name is Virgil Lovejoy, and I have two men followin' me with our furs. We're buffalo hunters. And you, Captain?" He saw the gold cord around the hat band and a brooch with crossed sabers. His Stetson was slapped up on the side like the Seventh Cavalry officers.

The captain looked at the stranger with puzzlement etched across his face. He shook his head to try to clear the cobwebs but to no avail. He still couldn't remember a thing.

"I'm afraid you have me at a disadvantage, sir," the captain replied. "It appears in the fall I've lost my memory." He stared at Virgil for a spell, then added, "I don't know who I am or what I'm even doing up here. I've apparently lost my horse. At least I still have my guns."

Lovejoy looked at the empty sleeve and the thousand-yard stare and instantly knew he had seen his share of battles. It was something one couldn't hide from someone who had gone through their own war, although it was for different causes.

"I've got coffee and some buffalo tongue iffin ya wanna share a meal with me," Virgil said. "It's the best part of the buff."

The captain stared at the stranger with a blank face, but he walked his way, using the cliff wall to keep his balance so he didn't tumble over the edge. His silver spurs jingled with every step. Virgil tied his horse to a rock, built a fire, and busied himself until the smell of fresh java and grilled meat filled the air.

Once the tongue was done, he forked it with a two-pronged stick he had whittled to points, passed it to the captain, and poked another for himself.

"Be careful, pilgrim." Virgil grinned. "It's so hot it'll burn your tongue." The Black man chuckled at his feeble attempt at humor.

Suddenly, the captain was famished. He couldn't remember when he'd last eaten. He couldn't even remember who he was. He bit into the delicacy and devoured two in minutes.

"It's kind of sweet, ain't it?" the captain said.

"Them tongues are worth six dollars a pound back east." Virgil grinned. He looked the captain over from head to toe and nodded. "In a spell, my two men are gonna ride in, so don't you take 'em for outlaws and shoot 'em or somethin'." Virgil grinned, showing a mouthful of white teeth. "I hear tell you cavalry boys are a tough lot and got happy trigger fingers."

"It would appear that I am a bit worse for wear," the captain said as he looked at his empty sleeve. He untied the bandana under his chin and felt the wound on his head.

"Once you've had a bit more to eat, let me look at the cut on your noggin. It looks like it needs tending to all proper like, or it'll get infected shore as shootin'." Virgil laughed. "And I bet them Indians fancy that blond hair a yours too." He pulled off his rabbit fur cap and showed the captain his short, curly hair. "They can hardly get ahold of mine. That's why I keep it so short."

Virgil laughed until he got a stitch, and despite all that had befallen the captain, he chuckled too. Virgil Lovejoy was an easy man to like.

Horses' hooves clacked on the hard trail, and sparks shot out from their shoes as they stepped on the stone. Virgil's horse whinnied, and Clinch's answered. Two burly men with long hair and hairy faces rode on horses with nine mules in tow.

"Step down, boys," Virgil said. "The coals are hot, and we've got sacks of tongue. This here is the captain. These are my men, sir. This here's my sidekick, Clinch West, and this is our hired hand, Bud Guns. They ain't dangerous or nothin', so you've got nothing to worry about."

"And you, Mr. Lovejoy?" the captain asked.

"And me what?" Virgil asked kindly.

"Where're your soldiers, Captain?" Bud snickered. Then he saw Virgil shoot him a dirty look, and he shut up.

The captain continued to look puzzled but replied, "Mighty fine to meet you both, gentlemen. Your boss here, Mr. Lovejoy, was kind enough to feed me. I'm afraid I had an accident." He lowered his head, and Clinch's chin fell to his chest, leaving his mouth open so wide two flies flew in.

"Why, I can see your brains," Bud huffed with wide eyes.

"Don't listen to him, Captain," Virgil said, looking at Guns as he showed him the back of his hand. "He's a danged fool. But I've got to admit I can see some bone up there. But there's no gray brains seeping out, so I figure it looks worse than it really is. You go ahead and clean up, and then we'll take a peek and see what we can do. I figure I can sew ya up, but we've got to clean the wound first. It ain't gonna be fun. Bud, give the captain some of that whiskey you spend the day sippin' on."

Bud frowned but knew better than to talk back to the boss, or he would get another backhand. He might knock his teeth out this time. So he passed the flask without a word.

"Thank you, Bud," the captain said. He finished his meal, and then he was ready to have his wound looked at. He dared not think what Virgil might find. He hoped his skull wasn't cracked, but his head throbbed so bad he wasn't sure.

"Have a look, Mr. Lovejoy," the captain said as he lowered his head.

Virgil whistled a long note and clicked his tongue. "Have a good swig of that rotgut, Captain. This is gonna sting like a hundred fire ants."

When Virgil cleaned the wound, he couldn't be hesitant. He knew he had to give it a deep scrub to make sure it was clean before he sewed the patch of scalp and yellow hair back onto his head. The whole time he cleaned the injury, the captain sat with a face carved in stone. Virgil noticed only the short breaths as the pain racked his body, but he heard not a peep from the officer. The one-armed stranger didn't even flinch when he sewed him up. When he was done, you could hardly see the stitches.

"I used wildcat gut," Virgil said. "That makes the best string to sew up a wound like that. It looks like you've seen a battle or two, Captain. I wonder what you was up to up here all by your lonesome. No offense intended, but it ain't normal to find an officer roamin' around the Rocky Mountains alone. You've got to admit it don't make much sense."

"Oh, I admit it makes no sense at all," the captain said. "I can't even remember a thing from this morning. The first I can remember was when I came to. I must have gotten knocked out. I had a horse because I saw the tracks, but ya can't see the bottom of that gorge with all those trees, so it could be down there with my supplies."

"I don't see how you're gonna get down that cliff," Clinch said. "Even if you did make it down, ya couldn't make it back up again, that's for danged sure. It's mighty steep all the way. It ain't worth the risk unless you was carryin' gold. Is that what you were doin'? Workin' some isolated vein?"

"Honestly, I have no idea what I was doing. I know my shirt and britches aren't Army issues. That puzzles me more than anything. Why am I wearing Indian clothing? The only thing I'm sure of is that I'm a captain of the US Cavalry. I don't know how I know it, but I do."

"There ain't a dad-gummed thing wrong with that," Virgil said. "Look at us; we all wear buckskins. It's the most practical clothes for the Rockies, and ya blend in a tad more. Maybe that's what you was doin'—trying not to be noticed. That's something that I know a lot about. What I can't figure out is, where's your soldiers?"

"That's true enough, but I doubt my apparel would be acceptable back at headquarters," the captain replied. "That's one of the mysteries that bothers me the most. Why am I dressed like some renegade? As far as my soldiers, I haven't seen any sign of them. You would think there'd be more hoofprints if I were with a patrol. All I've got are questions and not a single answer."

"Well, at least you're alive and not down in that gorge with your horse." Virgil smiled. He appeared to be a kind man but quick to anger. The captain noticed the way he'd looked at Bud. "I've heard of people losing their memory for a spell after a bad bang on the head. I bet in a day or two, you'll remember everything. At least, I hope so. Now you have my curiosity sparkin' like mad. You best come along with us, Captain. You'll have to walk, but we walk our horses half the time anyway. The trails are dangerous, and our horses ain't as surefooted as the mules."

"I would propose walking your horses and mules across that narrow trail and not all at the same time," the captain said. "It would appear that falling down the cliff isn't very appealing."

MEMORIES

THAT EVENING, THE CAPTAIN TOOK VIRGIL'S GENEROUS offer and spent the night with the buffalo hunters. They had elk with cornbread and gravy for dinner. A gallon kettle of coffee sat by the fire as bubbles popped from the spout, and the aroma filled the air. The sun vanished behind a massive mountain peak, and they plunged into darkness, and the temperatures cooled. Lighting bugs flashed in one place, only to disappear and light up elsewhere. Crickets played their symphony. The hunters tried to see into the pitch-black night every time they stopped. Paranoia still sat over them like a pesky fly.

Clinch West was even jumpier at night than on the trail riding drag. He pulled off his cap, scratched his mop of hair, and pulled on his long brown beard. All four men made sure they took care of their personals before it was dark. That was when men and animals in the wilderness were most vulnerable. Only a horse pooped and walked at the same time. The only illumination was the blanket of stars that rolled out as soon as the sun vanished. A ring of light surrounded the camp-fire, but beyond that was hard to penetrate. The flame's shadows danced on the captain's face as he stared at the fire and wondered who he really was. Would he ever find out?

The following morning, Virgil nudged the captain awake with the toe of his boot. He was standing over him with a rifle in his hand. For a second, the captain wondered if they were dangerous men after all, but when Lovejoy smiled in the dim light of the first crack of dawn, his teeth shined, and it reached his eyes. The captain let out a long breath.

"Are we already heading out?" the captain asked.

"It's another day to our hunting lodge," Virgil said. "It's where we store the hides when we're out shootin' more buffs. It's in a hard-to-find spot, so we haven't had a problem other than the bears."

"I thought we weren't gonna show anybody our hideout," Bud grumbled.

"Do you really think an Army captain with amnesia is here aimin' to steal our furs? If he was, he would probably have a more solid story than the one he's got." Virgil looked at the captain and added, "You've got to forgive Bud. He's not a bad fella, but he ain't too bright."

"I'm standin' right here beside ya, Virgil," Bud groused. "I ain't stupid, Mister Captain, sir. But you've got to admit this whole story you've told us is a bit farfetched, don't ya think?"

"I have to agree with Bud," the captain said, shaking his head. "Why, I don't even know my name."

"Come along, sir," Bud offered as he caved. "We're all saddled up and ready to go. There's one cup of coffee left in the kettle. We saved it for ya. Once you're done, hang it on the back of one of the mules 'cause it'll be hot."

Virgil smiled at Bud, and he grinned back.

"I told ya he was a decent fella." Virgil smiled. "He just needs to mature a little, and this is a hard place to choose for such a thing. But it is what it is. I'll get 'im through the season and back home with the Lord's help. Are you a religious man, Captain?"

"Why, I have no idea," the captain replied. "It would appear you are, sir."

"Not as much as I should be, but I do my best with what I was given, which wasn't much," Virgil said as he stared into the morning light like he was somewhere else. "If we don't stop, we'll be back at the lean-to before dark."

They traveled through the day at a brisk walk. It was true: most of the time, walking was safer, as the horses struggled with the muddy trails. The snow had melted, and the ground was still a little mushy. They only stopped once to water the horses in a spring and refill their water bags. Bud gave an extra one to the captain, who had nothing but his guns and a saber, boots, and a hat. All his belongings ended up at the bottom of the deep gorge.

Virgil didn't talk all day as he focused on their surroundings. He never missed a movement, but lucky for them, there were only elk and deer that startled and ran as soon as they saw the humans. They had some rugged miles to cover before dark, and they all took the challenge as serious as a funeral. The longer they were exposed with so many buffalo hides, the longer they were in danger of the local Indians stealing them, or worse. They might take a dislike to them for killing their food and shelter and make them pay the ultimate price.

Finally, as the end of the day approached, Virgil spoke. "We've made it, boys. It's just down the trail."

"I was sure the Crow Indians would be after us," Clinch said. "I can't believe nobody saw us with all the rifle fire."

"It's a big country," Virgil said. "The vastness makes men seem small, don't it?"

Bud nudged his horse and hurried for the shack. The captain supposed that was the right name for it. The cabin was ramshackle and cluttered—a burlap curtain billowed in the window with the morning breeze. The building looked worse for wear. The weeds and grass were overgrown and consuming the porch. The floor sagged, as did the roof, and it was stripped of paint. No one had maintained the small hunter's shack for years. They saw no need since they only used it in the spring and summer. It was so grown over the captain didn't notice it in the foliage until he was right on top of it.

When Virgil pulled the sagging door open, it was dark, damp, and full of cobwebs. It hadn't seen sunlight for a week. Obviously, this was a temporary place to stay while they hunted buffalo for their valuable hides.

"You certainly picked a choice spot to hide your shack," the captain said. "I didn't see it until I nearly bumped into it."

"It's more like a hovel, but it keeps us warm on the summer nights and dry when it rains. It don't look like much because that's the way I planned it. How many outlaws do you see botherin' to rob poor folk? I ain't heard of none. It almost looks abandoned, don't it?"

"That's a clever move," the captain said. "I've seen you with your Bible. Do you read a lot?"

"I must say, I sure do try, but when you set yourself a high bar in your work, you'll have to answer. That's what seems to take most of my time and pert near all my Sundays. I, sir, am somewhat of a perfectionist when it comes to work, but when it comes to going to church, I unfortunately procrastinate. I hope I change my ways before I stand before the pearly gates to answer to my maker. But in the meantime, I keep my Good Book here in my shirt close to my heart, so I'll never forget my good fortune."

"I could use some good fortune right now." The captain frowned.

"I'd say you've already had a good dose, Captain." Virgil smiled. "You survived when your horse didn't. If that's not good fortune, I don't know what is. It all depends on how you tend to look at things. My cup always seems to be half full, and you think yours is half empty, but that ain't true at all. Iffin ya wait long enough, there's some good in everything that happens, pilgrim. That's why patience is a virtue—especially to a wise man."

In minutes, Clinch had the fire burning and started making supper while Bud began unsaddling the horses, hobbling them, and brushing them down. Virgil dug through the pack mule's supplies and found blankets to make a bedroll for the captain. Soon, the smell of fried bacon filled the air as the birds' chatter quieted with the vanishing sun. As Virgil sat on a lightning-racked tree stump, he read by the light of the flickering flames, which cast dancing shadows on his dark face. He traced his finger under the words, and his lips silently moved.

Occasionally, he stopped and pondered what he had read, then resumed his studies.

Everybody was busy but the captain. It made him uneasy doing nothing, so he jumped in and helped Bud care for the horses. He checked their shoes for damage after covering such a rough country. There was plenty of pasture grass for the three horses to feed on. When they were done, Bud slapped the captain on the back and smiled. Like Virgil said, Guns wasn't a bad guy. He was just a little slow to catch on to things.

"I wonder how I'm gonna find a horse up here," the captain said once they were done and sitting around the fire eating strips of greasy bacon. "I've got money. I found two double eagles in my vest pocket."

"It ain't wise to go tellin' strangers how much money ya got on ya," Virgil cautioned. "For us, twenty dollars ain't all that much considering our hides and tongues, but not everybody that comes up here does well. It's best to keep your money count to yourself, Captain. Heck, just look at Bud's eyes. When you mentioned money, they nearly popped out of his head."

"I ain't a thief," Bud Guns retorted. "You know better than that, Virgil."

"We all know you're an honest man, although lazy," Virgil said. "But not everybody in the Rockies is like us, Bud."

That night, the captain slept restlessly. His ordeal when he lost his horse and the long and fast two-day trek to the hunter's shack had left him exhausted, but his mind still wandered. Three men snored as Lovejoy continued to read his Bible into the night. It was hard to tell if the Black man ever slept. He seemed to be on watch every time the captain awoke with a start during the night. He kept having a dream in which he lost his memory, only to wake up and find it wasn't a dream but the hard truth. He still couldn't remember a thing.

The following day, the captain was up an hour before the break of dawn. He quietly built a fire in the adobe cooker in the back and made a kettle of piping hot coffee. The porch was void of chairs, so he sat on the edge with his feet dangling over the side. Steam rolled from the cup and the captain's breath. It was chilly before the sun came up. When it did break over the horizon, a prism of colors accompanied the orange disk. It appeared as though it was reeled into the sky by some giant pulley in the heavens. Long shadows stood to the west as it broke over the mountains. He turned his face to the rays and let them warm his face. For an instant, he forgot his problem and basked in the glory of Mother Nature.

When Virgil sat beside him on the side of the porch, he didn't make a sound. The captain was startled by his sudden appearance. When he looked up, his locked eyes with Lovejoy's. There appeared to be some deep knowledge of humankind that the captain couldn't fathom. He had clearly seen more than the officer.

"Do you always sneak up on people like that?" the captain asked.

"Yep," Lovejoy answered but didn't elaborate.

The captain stared at the man who'd saved him and given him a temporary direction. He had provided him with food, shelter, and what seemed to be a smidgen of friendship.

After a long silence, the captain finally asked, "Yep,

what? Why do you do it if you know you startle a man? That may be a good way to get shot."

"I don't do it often," Virgil admitted. "But when I do, it gives me a moment to see a man's face before he puts on a mask. Sometimes, sad people play happy all the time, but the secret is always in their eyes if you catch them unaware. It's the only time you can see a man's true feelings. I thought I'd take a risk on you, Captain. I can't help but believe I was put on your path for a reason. Our meeting is just too unusual to be something other than a small miracle. Anyway, the important thing is you safe now."

"But I have no memories," the captain said. "None at all."

"If that happened to me, it would be a blessing as long as I didn't lose my skills or instinct," Virgil said. His voice sounded like an ocean breeze. "Some folks don't have the good fortune to have a pleasant past. Maybe your past ain't as good as you expect it to be. A man with expectations is a man headin' for disappointment."

"I really hadn't thought about it that way," the captain replied. "Since I'm in the middle of the wilderness without a single soldier, that isn't exactly a good sign."

"I was just thinkin' the same thing, pilgrim." Lovejoy smiled.

He pulled an old corncob pipe from his large frontiersman's pocket along with a twist of tobacco. He chopped up enough to fill the bowl, popping it in his mouth as he fished for a match.

"Fancy a smoke, Captain?" Virgil asked. "Do you remember if you smoke or not? You would think that would be instinctive iffin ya did."

"As a matter of fact, I do believe I smoke." The Army man pulled a fancy ceramic pipe from his pocket. "But it appears I'm fresh out of tobacco. It must have gone over the cliff with my saddlebags." He tapped his pockets to make sure.

"Here, have some of mine," Virgil replied as he fired up his bowl and puffed until his head was in a smoky cloud, challenging to see.

They sat silently for the next hour until they heard Clinch West and Bud Guns wake up and begin to bang tin cups and plates.

"You boys fancy some breakfast?" Bud called out from the makeshift kitchen. "I'm makin' fryin' pan biscuits, and we've got bacon from yesterday's supper."

"Bring the table and chairs out, Clinch!" Virgil yelled from the porch. "We don't need to eat on the floor today. We can eat at a proper table."

"How is that missin' arm workin' out for ya, sir?" Virgil asked. "That must be a burr under the saddle for a military man."

He looked down at his empty sleeve and said, "It doesn't seem to bother me too much. I've hardly noticed, so I must have lost it a spell back."

"You look like an Indian fighter," Virgil ventured. "Your buckskins are well cured and sewed by somebody with skill. I reckon you've run into some mountain men up here or somethin'. I don't know what happened but if I ponder on it long enough, I might get a vision."

"Get a vision?" the captain replied, surprised. "Are you some sort of mystic?"

"Oh, heavens no." Virgil laughed. "I'm just a simple man who sometimes sees things that make me believe something higher has a hand in what happens."

The captain smiled but didn't say more.

"Let me have a gander at that hole in your head," Virgil said. "We don't want it to get infected."

CROW WEDDING

AFTER LEVI AND DAHTESTE HAD RODE INTO THE compound and surprised his friends, the mountain men and the Crow women sat on the porch as was the custom in the compound at the end of each day. Angus prepared coffee as the sun neared the mountain peaks, and the air began to cool. Rusty Steel was staring at the newlywed couple like he was chewing on crow and was having a hard time swallowing. Levi knew that his old friend—the very man who'd brought him to the Rockies when he and the captain had been heading west—had a bone to pick with him.

Portland Pete and Yosemite Bob were pitching pennies against the side of the cabin. The last rays of sun lit up the upper part of the building as the lower half fell into the shadows.

"That's a leaner!" Pete laughed. "I told ya I'd beat ya, Bob. That's eight cents you owe me."

"How can you even see it from here?" Bob grumbled. "Don't you touch that before I have a look."

Syracuse Sam brought out a cast iron pan. When he

pulled off the lid, they saw a dozen baked apples covered in brown sugar and cinnamon. Steam rose off the hot fruit and filled the air, mixing with the aroma of fresh coffee. The rest of the mountain men and the Crow women sat around the family table. It was clear Rusty had a bone to pick. It showed by the way he pouted his lips and stared at Levi with questioning eyes. He finally frowned.

"You still haven't told me why you two didn't wait until I came back from the mountains to get hitched," Rusty huffed. "And here I thought I was your mentor, Levi. Why, I should have been your best man, youngin'. I've been like a father to you."

"I'm afraid we didn't have a say-so in the matter, and the Indians don't have best men like we do. Crow weddings ain't like ours." Levi smiled, but now he wasn't so sure of himself. "Your blood brother, Chief Hachta, said we had to get hitched, and it wasn't a question either. Later, I found out a couple of disgruntled warriors braves were at the root of the hurry. He wanted to stop trouble before it started."

"I ain't ever been to a wedding," Rusty said. "At least not an Indian wedding. How about you two tell me all about it." He fixed his eyes on Dahteste.

"You want me to tell you?" she asked in Crow.

"Yes, ma'am, but I want you to tell me in English. Levi, Angus, and me learned Crow, so you've got to learn to speak English iffin you wanna live in this compound." Rusty smiled, and his eyes twinkled with mischief. "Levi told me you was workin' on your language skills, so you might as well get used to it. There's nothin' like practice to make it perfect."

Everybody was on Angus's porch having an afternoon coffee after work. Of course, once done, McFarlin would go back to his chores until he was dozing on his feet, but the rest of the men were done for the day. Levi and Dahteste sat on the porch glider swinging to the rhythm of the locusts that chattered in the trees. The Crow woman's eyes grew softer as she pouted, but she wouldn't get her way.

Levi had already discovered how she manipulated men with her beauty. He also knew she had a warrior's mind and was hard as coffin nails when put to the test. Still, he liked that Rusty had been the one to oblige her to make an effort. He was an essential friend to her chief, and she knew she couldn't say no.

"How about if I kick things off so it'll be easier for you to get goin'?" Levi said. "It is true you're the only one of us that wasn't there, Rusty. Everybody in the tribe attended—everybody in the compound too. I never in my wildest dreams expected such a thing to happen. We were both caught by surprise. I figure old Chief Hachta did it to cool off the other suitors. Dahteste appeared to have had quite a following, but she turned each and every one down. Except for me, and I hadn't even gotten around to asking her to jump the broom. It kind of snuck up on us without warning. Before we knew it, drums were echoing all across the mountains. Then, once we arrived, the flutes started. It was quite an affair."

"You don't know how to tell the story, Levi Johnson," Dahteste grumbled. "It was not an affair. It is a wedding. At our wedding, we danced the snake dance and the crow-hop. Every part of the wedding is essential. Remember when I poured water into your hands from mine?" She looked at Levi with raised eyebrows. "We were washing away our memories and making ourselves pure. It cleans our past mis-judg-ments." She had difficulty saying the word.

"Where did y'all have the wedding?" Rusty asked.

Now, he was more curious than put out. He knew he couldn't expect them to wait on him. He hadn't even known when he would return. But still, he had hacking rights just the same.

"Under the sacred peaks of those mountains above us," Dahteste replied and smiled. "In the Crow peoples' sacred temple—Mother Nature.

"Then we walked the Rite of Seven Steps," Dahteste continued. "These were our wedding vows. Levi took one step around the sacred fire and made a vow and gave me a gift; then I made the next step, giving him a present, until we made all seven passes and vows. Levi gave me ears of dried corn, which represent fertility. I gave him an eagle's feather, which stands for loyalty, and a stone that symbolizes strength. As we took our vows, the tribe gathered around us in a big circle."

Levi nodded as she spoke. He was amazed at how fast she learned everything about him and his language. He could hardly believe it.

"I get a sneakin' suspicion you've been practicin' behind my back." Levi laughed. "You've been puttin' on like you were havin' trouble learnin' English. I reckon you've tricked us all."

"Chief Hachta has been teaching me," Dahteste confessed, her face flushed red. "He's the only one in our stronghold that speaks good English," she admitted with smiling eyes. "It was my surprise to you and your friends. Especially Rusty Steel, the chief's blood brother."

"Well, go on with the wedding story." Rusty grinned. "It couldn't have ended there. I know the Crow people; when they have an excuse to have a pow-wow, they make the best of it."

He was already hooked on the story. He closed his eyes and imagined every detail. He knew the Crow Indians better than anyone in the compound, along with Angus, who had an Indian wife too. Still, only Rusty was a full-blown blood brother to a chief.

"We made a fire circle using stones and seven different types of wood. Inside the circle of rocks was a large pile of ceremonial firewood. This is left unlit as a smaller fire to the north and another to the south burn. These two separate fires represent our individual lives before we are joined in marriage. Once the smaller fires were burning, Levi and I pushed the burning wood into the main pile, igniting the large fire. When the fires merged, we were as one. This is how we were married."

"You should have seen all the food," Angus said. "It was a feast fit for a king."

Pine Needle sat beside her husband at the large table. She had come for a few days to give Dahteste moral support because she had never lived with non-Indian people. But she quickly saw that Dahteste didn't need any help. Then again, she was a war chief, and Angus's wife's skills were curing skins.

―――――

LATER THAT EVENING, when Pine Needle and Dahteste were making the tipi ready to be occupied again, Rusty and Levi sat on the porch alone. Johnson had waited intentionally until everyone left to have a private word with his friend. Some things he felt were better kept on the hush. He didn't want to seem to be prying into Forrester's personal business. He had been a good friend despite their completely different backgrounds. He had overcome every challenge, including losing his arm. Levi had never had a friend like him before. He didn't intend to lose his friendship just because he got married.

"I've been meanin' to ask about Will Forrester," Levi said. "How'd he take to me runnin' off with Dahteste? I reckon that wrecked our plans, all right. I feel bad about how it happened so fast and all. I wanted to talk to him to let him know our friendship don't change just because I'm married."

"Oh, you know how Will is," Rusty replied. "He hardly ever lets anybody know what he's really thinkin'. You used to be like that too, but now you've changed, pilgrim. When you got here, you were more like Forrester. The Comanche had made you hard. But you take to the mountains like eggs to chickens. It's natural for ya."

"Did Will take off right after the wedding?" Levi asked.

"Yep," Rusty confirmed. "He left just a spell after. He said he wanted to find himself like I did when I disappeared last winter. I know it did me a world of good, but for some men, it may be better not to find their true selves until they're ready. I ain't so sure the captain's ready."

"And you ain't heard anything from him at all?" Levi asked. "Not even in the Indian gossip?"

"Not a word, but don't you worry." Rusty smiled. "If anybody can take care of himself against hostiles and road bandits, it's the captain. I reckon he's done like I did and headed for an unknown country—for us, anyway. I doubt there be many places where one Indian tribe or another ain't been with them bein' here hundreds of years. Heck, we just got here, and White folks are already creatin' a ruckus everywhere they go. Some come and feel they be entitled to anything they want. That confuses the Indians. Heck, it confuses me too."

"I still worry about Will," Levi said. "When we left Kansas, we had big plans for the future, and no matter how hard we tried, things didn't work out for squat. I reckon it's that old friend destiny that moved us about like blind ducks."

"You know worry never changed the outcome of nothin'. I've always believed that a man makes his own destiny, but there are a lot of curves on the road to make one lose his way. Maybe we all have a bunch of possible destinies in us, and depending on the decisions we make, one or another affects ya."

"How long were you gone on your soul-searching journey?" Levi asked.

"When you take a trip like that, it's only for one person," Rusty whispered like it was a secret. "It's for the man takin' it and nobody else. That's why I don't talk about it. The only other person that knows all that happened on my soul-seeking journey is Dog, and he ain't talkin'." Rusty smiled. It was true he had kept the details of his trek a secret. He hadn't even told anybody where he disappeared to. "I felt like a new man after a good spell of traveling alone. I reckon the captain needed something like that to figure out where he fits in this mysterious life we live so far from civilization."

"Them's a lot of words for not answering my question." Levi smiled. "How long were ya gone?"

"I reckon it was from early winter to the first thaw," Rusty said. "You know I don't give dates and such much attention. I can't even remember my age, and it ain't due to forgetfulness. It simply has no importance to me, so why go to the trouble of remembering somethin' for nothin'?"

"I have half a mind to try to go and find him," Levi mused. "Something's eatin' at my stomach, and it's givin' me a bad feelin'."

"You just got married." Rusty laughed until he got a stitch. "That's a feelin' that's gonna sit with ya for a spell, pilgrim, and it ain't 'cause the captain's in trouble. It's 'cause you just got hitched, and with an Indian woman. Why, I'd be scared to death. Especially marrying a war chief." He laughed so hard that tears streamed down his cheeks.

HOSTILE INDIANS

AFTER BREAKFAST, THE BUFFALO HUNTERS GOT AN unexpected and unwanted surprise. For the first time since they arrived in the Rockies, they saw an abundance of human footprints, and they weren't made by boots. The captain dropped to one knee and studied the tracks.

"Indians," the captain whispered. "There's no way for me to tell how old the tracks are, but I'd say they're probably from yesterday at the latest. They might even be from last night or early this morning. Since the local Indians know the area like the back of their hands, they must have moved in the dark without us noticing. As a rule, hostiles usually attack an hour or two before first light. I doubt they missed our smell or our fire. Now, we better tread lightly."

"How do you know all about Indians but can't remember who you are?" Bud Guns asked. "You'd have thought you would have forgotten all that too."

"You don't forget some things," Clinch declared. "Just because you lose your memory don't mean you can't remember how to pee. You're dumber than a marble in a tin can. He said he lost his memory, not his mind."

"I'm a danged sight smarter than you, buster," Bud retorted. You could see in his eyes that he believed he was brighter than West. It almost made the captain smile, but not quite.

"I wonder where they've left their horses," Virgil said. "They might be spyin' on us right now."

The group of trappers decided to ride a few circles around the shack to make sure there were no new tracks, but that was precisely what they found.

"I reckon we've found the horses because those tracks are from Indian ponies," the captain said. "I'd say there are a dozen warrior braves on their mounts. They're moving quick, so they must have someplace in mind. I wonder what tribe they're from."

"What's it matter?" Bud asked. "A hostile Indian is a Indian. They all be dangerous. If I never run into an Indian, it'll be too soon for me."

"That's not really true," the captain replied. He didn't know how he knew, but he did. It was something inside. "There are good people here in the mountains with the Indians just like there are good and bad White men up here and even back in civilization, though I would suppose most White men in these mountains are ne'er-do-wells."

"I beg your pardon," Clinch West growled. "I take offense to that."

"Excuse me, gentlemen," the captain said. "Present company excluded."

"Exclu-what?" Bud Guns asked.

"Not countin' us, stupid," Clinch replied. "Everybody except us is what he's sayin'."

"You best be careful who you call stupid, fool," Bud threatened.

"And what are ya gonna do about it?" Clinch asked.

"Stop it right now," Virgil suddenly growled, and both men's eyes locked on their leader. "You two quibble like a couple of youngins. When are ya gonna grow up? You'll have to excuse my friends, Captain. They're always bickerin'. But it's just their way. They ain't bad, fellas. Clinch is my right-hand man."

This brought another frown from Bud Guns. He was obviously jealous and stupider than he appeared. But he was a great shot with a rifle if a man could get him to do what he was told. He was the kind of dumb person who thought they were more intelligent than the rest when they were utterly ignorant. The only one he appeared to listen to was Virgil, but then again, the captain suspected everyone who met Mr. Lovejoy listened to what he had to say. You felt his presence as soon as he walked into the campfire. It was almost like an electrical shock.

"It's all between the ears," Clinch said as he tapped his temple with his finger then stopped to spit into a peach can. "That's right—between the ear holes. That's where your brains should have been."

The captain daydreamed for a moment and wondered: if he rode the world cleaning up the vermin, might it earn him the smallest measure of thanks for making the world a better place upon his ultimate judgment before his maker? He had no memory, but he felt in his very core what he was. He was a soldier, even if he couldn't remember his name. That much he knew, but not only from the traces of an officer's uniform.

He knew what he felt inside. It all seemed so clear despite the puzzling situation. He wondered if he'd had this clear vision of his future before he lost his memory to amnesia and the fall. He still didn't remember what happened, but deduction gave the apparent answer. He had fallen off his horse, or it had maybe even fallen on him. That would be why every bone in his body ached, but he refused to show it. His ribs only hurt severely when he laughed, and there was little to laugh about.

"Are you all right, Captain?" Virgil asked. "You've got a faraway look about ya. Has your memory come back?"

He realized he was staring into the distance with a thousand-yard stare. "No, sir, but despite losing my memory, I believe I'm going to be all right, even if it doesn't come back."

"To be honest, we ain't come across soldier one since we started shootin' buffs," Virgil said. "Heck, we ain't even seen any Indians till now. For the life of me, I can't figure out what you were doin' way up here. I reckon you could go find one of the frontier forts back in Kansas. They must know who you be, sir."

"You don't have to call me sir, Virgil. I'm not your captain. I believe you probably saved my life, so I should be the one calling you sir."

"Oh, I doubt you'd have perished if we hadn't run into ya," Lovejoy said. "You seem like a rugged fella to me. Honestly, I've been callin' ya sir for lack of something else to call ya. I reckon Captain will have to do until you locate someone you know, which I find doubtful way the heck up here. That, or your memory comes back. I'm afraid that memory loss ain't one of my specialties."

"I suppose I'll have to live for today and not ponder yesterday." Forrester laughed. "Since I don't know where I'm goin', I don't have to worry about tomorrow. All I've got to do is focus on today."

"That's the spirit, Captain," Virgil said. "Yesterday's gone anyway, and the future is only real if you make it there, and that's always a throw of the dice. I've always believed the best way to live is for the moment. If there's no past, there are no bad memories. And if there's no future, we have no expectations, so we avoid disappointments. I could use a little bit of whatever you've got."

"From where I'm standing, I don't see I have a choice." The captain smiled, and it reached his eyes. "Maybe it will all work out for the best, but if I was on my own, where's my patrol? An officer rarely leaves the forts without a proper escort."

He liked Virgil, and he believed if it wasn't for his unexpected appearance, he might have lost direction or made another mistake that would have cost him his life. Now, he even had shelter if it rained, and food. For some reason, the captain smiled. He felt like it was the first time in a long while. It wasn't a hint of a smile, but it was broad and stretched his face. He almost felt like he had been given a new life. In a way, he had. It would have been a different story if he had gone over with his horse.

They returned to the shack and checked their weapons for dry powder and prepared to be attacked. They had no idea if the Indians were still around, but if they weren't ready and the Indians showed up, they would be slaughtered. Bud's face glistened with sweat, and when he swallowed, his Adam's apple bobbed up and down like a fishing cork. His mouth was so dry, his lips stuck to his front teeth. Of the four, he was the one most afraid. Still, he held his rifle to his shoulder and waited like everybody else. Just because he was frightened, it didn't make him a coward.

Strangely enough, the captain felt elation. He was looking forward to what was to come, and he wasn't even sure why. Despite his missing arm, he never let on but acted like he didn't even notice it was gone. He handled himself with calm and deliberate control. He was apparently an officer's officer. He still couldn't figure out the buckskins, but he was sure there was a simple explication.

What puzzled him the most was why he was in the Rocky Mountains far from any frontier forts. Still, somehow, he knew he was an Indian fighter. That would explain a lot of the puzzle, for one thing, his dress. He had seen other frontier officers dressed so, at least he thought he had, though he didn't know why and couldn't remember who they were, where it was, or even what they looked like. Somehow, he just knew, was all.

The first cloud of arrows came down like slanted rain from the heavens. They couldn't even see the archers, but the arrows were real enough. So many stuck into the lean-to, it looked like a porcupine. But the shack held and protected the four men from the shower of death. They knew next would come the warrior braves with guns.

Bullets began to slam into the wood plank sides of the shack. Splinters exploded as chunks of lead burrowed deep into the timber. The bullets didn't penetrate the thick planks. Still, they couldn't see anybody, but Bud got nervous and shot off a round. His eyes were as big as saucers.

"Don't shoot until I tell you to!" the captain ordered.

There was no denying what he wanted. He was apparently in charge. Even Virgil was waiting to see what the Army man would have them do next. He felt he would know how to proceed better than anybody. None of the trappers had ever fought hostile Indians. The first sign they saw were a few feathers poking over the buffalo grass. The captain pointed to the plume and nodded. Four rifle shots rang out simultaneously. All four feathers disappeared. The buffalo hunters were as good a shot as they had claimed.

"I count eight of 'em left," the captain said as he pulled his saber. "Wait here. I'll be right back."

Before the hunters could reply, the captain vanished. He seemed to disappear into the shadows and didn't make a single sound as he left. Now, all three hunters had half-moons of sweat under their arms as the tension built. The sun climbed higher and bore down in waves of heat. Even Virgil was nervous. Eight Indians were still an awful lot of enemies, and they obviously had the better position. Plus, this was probably their backyard.

They had the advantage with cap and ball rifles. The only edge the hunters had was they were crack shots, and the Indians probably weren't. Bullets cost money, but the hunters had spent days practicing from above the buffalo herds. That, and they could reload and get three shots off in a minute. This, too, took long hours of practice but was a buffalo hunter's bread and butter.

They all heard an Indian begin to sing, but his song was cut short. The buffalo hunters' faces were full of questions, and their eyes were spread wide. Minutes passed, and then a half hour, which stretched into an hour. Still, they had no idea what was going on. All they had clear was that the captain hadn't returned, so things didn't look good. They knew they would be easy pickings if the Indians could dispatch the captain without a single shot. But what were the Indians waiting for? Why didn't they attack and get it over with? The passing of time was so slow it felt like the captain had been gone all day. As each minute ticked by, the odds of him making it back were smaller and smaller.

Movement was visible, for instants, between tall trees. Two gunshots rang out, and Bud went to shoot. Virgil grabbed his barrel just in time and forced it toward the ground. The bullet dug a hole in the dirt not four yards away.

"Stop, shootin', for Pete's sake. You're gonna kill the captain," Virgil snarled. "Now, don't you dare shoot that gun again until I tell ya, or I'm gonna wing ya myself. Do you understand, Mr. Guns?"

Bud nervously nodded. Now, he was more afraid of Virgil than the Indians. He figured the captain was already toast anyway, so worrying about him made no sense. Just the same, he followed orders. Virgil was the only man he listened to.

THE CAPTAIN

As soon as the captain ducked into the dense foliage under a stand of trees, he dropped to the ground, waiting a moment to listen for out-of-place sounds. It was too quiet. Even the locusts and crickets had ceased their concertos. It wouldn't do to run into a warrior or two trying to do the same to them. He used mud to darken the gleam of his saber so rays of light wouldn't reflect and give his position away, ruining his plans. Surprise was elemental to his attack. He hoped to go for the Indians from behind, driving them into the sights of the buffalo hunters as they fled his wrath.

The captain stopped and thought for a moment. He didn't know why he had run off on his own. He wondered if his plan was too bold and if he had bitten off more than he could chew. He couldn't remember skirmishes in the past, but he knew the memories were there, locked away in his mind somewhere. He could feel them like scars on his soul. Would he ever remember the past again? At this point, he didn't have the slightest idea, but he knew he had to focus on the moment and put his problems aside so he could concentrate on what he was doing.

His missing arm was a constant reminder of war. He assumed he didn't lose it by being run over by a train. He felt his blood begin to heat up like it had a life of its own. Despite the tension, he was calm as a millpond. The soft beat of his heart could barely be heard between his ears. His breathing was long and easy. Yet, his deep-blue, piercing eyes looked like they were full of electricity, like two bolts of lightning. They narrowed as his brow furrowed. Beads of sweat popped up through the mud caked on his face. It made his stare all the scarier as hackles raised on his neck. It was now or never.

He threw caution to the wind and disregarded the enemy's numbers. The captain pulled his knife and stuck it between his teeth. All four pistols were primed and ready in his leather belt. His saber hung from his side. If he made it that far, he would use the sword and, finally, the knife. If the Indian warriors weren't dead by then, he would use it on himself. He knew deep down inside he couldn't let the hostiles capture an Indian fighter. They would make him suffer a week of torture as they skinned him alive one strip at a time.

When the captain drew close enough to smell the enemy, he crawled on his belly, carefully choosing his path, making sure he didn't move a blade of grass or a branch of leaves. He heard whispers in a language that somehow seemed familiar. He could even pick out some words. It made him wonder what other surprises awaited him. He instantly knew they were Crow Indians.

He had no idea how he knew, but he recognized

their language. He knew they would be dangerous, but he somehow knew he had faced men even more fierce than these young warriors. They probably had seen all the buffalo hides and were out to steal them. It would take them a month of Sundays to make such a kill. Now, their greed might cost them their lives.

Once the soldier was behind their hobbled horses, he cut their ropes, quietly slapped their rumps, and silently made wild gestures, so they ran away. Still, the only sound was that of shoeless ponies walking on soft mossy ground. He left the only horse tied to a tree. He would use it later if he survived. The officer crawled with an arm and a stump to where the enemy lay in wait. Hopefully, he would get close enough to strike before they attacked Virgil and his men again. It would make all the difference in success and defeat. If they did attack, he would probably be killed by the White men's bullets. They were good shots, but they would be shooting at anything moving in a rush attack.

The officer covered his face with dirt and stuffed his yellow hair into his hat. He hoped to scare them enough for them to hesitate an instant. That millisecond would be all he needed to get the edge. They also had to swing their heavy rifle barrels one hundred and eighty degrees. If he was quick, he could kill four before they could counterattack.

The scream came from someplace deep inside the Army officer and passed through gritted teeth. It sounded full of danger and pain—like a wounded animal from another time and place. As he ran, thin branches and leaves slapped him in the face. Rivulets of blood ran down his brow where thorny bushes scratched his forehead and cheeks. His eyes were spread wide and looked crazed. He pulled a pistol while drawing back the hammer and pulled the trigger in a blast, a flash of fire, and a puff of smoke. He dropped the first gun and had already pulled the second as he slipped his finger into the trigger guard. Again, it bucked in his hand.

The captain stood there like he was invincible, totally exposed, in the open. Another gunshot and the smell of gunpowder. A third and fourth bullet thundered toward the Crow. One had just managed to turn toward the madman when he was shot in the chest. His eyes crossed, and the air emptied from his lungs as blood pooled beneath his body.

He looked past the last Crow warriors toward his new friends. Luckily, they hadn't opened fire. Now, he had to finish this. He drew his saber, but the remaining Indians ran for their lives. They didn't even recognize their aggressor as a White man with his face covered in mud and blood. As he waved to the buffalo hunters, four men lay dead beside his feet. It was over.

Virgil cautiously walked toward the dead Crow warriors with his gun in his fist. West and Guns followed closely behind. It had all happened so quickly that they couldn't believe they had survived. They looked at the captain like he was a man from another world. The mud on his face, mixed with sweat and blood, ran down his neck and shirt.

"Are ya hit, Captain?" Virgil asked. "I only heard four pistol shots, and the hostiles were shootin' rifles. I reckoned that was you, weren't it?" He looked at the gunshot men on the ground. "You slaughtered 'em, sir. I doubt they had a chance in hell of fighting you off."

"I ain't ever seen nothin' like it, Captain," said an

awed Clinch West. "And this ain't the first Indians I've come across."

"I ain't even heard of nothin' like it, sir," Bud said. He had just gotten a new hero alongside Virgil.

"Well, some of them got away, so we can't stay here any longer," the captain said. "They'll have fathers, brothers, and uncles who won't like us killing their boys. They had no business out here. They were far too green to try what they did. I doubt they would have taken you men even if I wasn't here."

"I ain't so sure about that, Captain." Virgil smiled. His white teeth contrasted with his brown skin.

"We'd have been dead meat by now, believe me," Clinch said. "Why, I'm still a little shaky and all."

"I'm all ears, Captain," Virgil said. "If you say it's time to cut and run, then off we go. I believe, just like you, that someone is gonna come back here to take those boys' bodies home, and they'll be lookin' for us too. It ain't worth a few more buffalo skins. We've got more than we ever imagined anyway, so it's best iffin we ain't here when they arrive."

"Let's see if we can keep ahead of them while we're getting out of these mountains," the captain said. "Soon, every Indian in the Rockies will know we're here."

"Don't get me wrong, sir," Bud Guns said. "I apologize for actin' like a smart aleck and all, but now I admire you, Captain. But how do you know these are Crow Indians if you can't remember nothin'? I'm havin' a hard time wrappin' my head around how that amnesia stuff works."

"If and when I figure it out, you'll be the first to know, Bud. That I promise. I guess I've had contact with Crow Indians before. I understood a few words they said when I crawled up on them when they had their backs to me."

"Why, I'd be scared to death if I had to do somethin' like that," Clinch said. "You're the bravest man I've ever seen."

"Bravest?" the captain asked, chuckling. "Craziest is probably more like it."

They all had the kind of nervous laugh that sometimes comes after acts of extreme violence. Blowflies buzzed around the fresh bodies as buzzards circled in the air above. The scavengers had already located the corpses and were only waiting for the humans to leave. Crows lined the trees as they cawed accusingly. It sounded like they were yelling for the intruders to get out. It was time for them to feed.

Two hours later, the mules were packed and the horses saddled. The captain took the only sizable horse in the war party. It was a mustang, full of spunk and vinegar. It was the perfect mount for the memory-less captain. He thought he might just keep it. It suited him right down to the ground. They quietly began their descent from the buffalo-killing fields to the Yellowstone Valley below. Then they would be halfway out of danger. They would have left the Crow land and stepped on the Blackfeet Indian's domain. That would be a whole other can of worms.

Saddles squeaked, and horses blew as the mules groaned under the weight. They traveled hard all day, hardly stopping except to water the animals and fill their water skins. Due to rugged switchback trails, they had to walk their horses half the time. Virgil was good with directions, and he'd remembered landmarks on the way up, which they used now to descend the higher mountains where only Indian hunters ventured. There, the buffalo were plentiful in the hidden valleys. The officer wondered how the buffalo found such lush places.

The captain saw the trail in his mind like it was an internal map. Once Lovejoy had given him the directions, the captain rode ahead of the party to ensure the trail was safe and no hostiles were waiting in ambush. They knew the Indians couldn't be that quick, but he knew they had speedy methods of communication. He looked into the sky as soon as the thought entered his mind. He saw the smoke signals overhead, and they could be seen for miles.

"Look up there," the captain said as he stared at the sky. "The Crow Indians already know what happened. That smoke up there is a message to sound the alert. I just hope we aren't between their camp and the warriors that ran away. Come on, finish filling those goat skins, and let's get back on the trail. We're wasting valuable light. We'll have to stop for the night, but I doubt the Crow will sleep tonight. They'll know this country well enough to avoid the dangers, and we don't."

"We'll have to sleep in turns," Virgil said, "while two of us keep watch. It'll be risky for the Indians to hit us at night without light from a fire. It would be too easy to make a mistake and lose a bunch of braves."

"Tonight, we can't risk a fire," the captain said. "We'll have to eat the stale biscuits from this morning. It's imperative we keep our bodies fed, or we won't have enough energy to outrun the Crow."

"Impera-what?" Bud asked.

"Necessary, and ya can't do without, dummy." Clinch

snickered. "I'd buy ya a dictionary, but ya don't know how to read."

"Shush now before you wake the dead," the captain said as he looked all around and then jumped onto the mustang. "I'll see you boys in a few hours. I wanna make sure the Crow didn't pass us last night, and they're not out there somewhere waiting to bushwhack us."

The captain sniffed the air like a dog, then he wheeled the horse around and rode down the trail bareback like he'd ridden that way all his life. Dust corkscrewed behind the hammering hooves as he crossed the green valley and disappeared over a rise in the land. Clinch and Bud exchanged looks. They couldn't hide their fear like Virgil and the captain could.

They weren't even sure the captain ever got scared. Not with the way he went at those Indians. Even the buffalo hunters were shocked to see sudden death like that. It vibrated right down to their souls. Maybe the captain was darker than they thought—they sure as heck didn't plan to cross him. Lucky for them, they were friends.

THE HUNT

"Time seems to stand still out here, like a snake in the sun, layin' across the road," Rusty said when he looked up from his Good Book.

Besides the chatter of birds in the trees and woodpeckers hammering out some strange Morse code, everything was quiet in the compound.

Rusty looked toward the tipi and noticed smoke coming out of the vent. Still, he hadn't heard anybody stir. But it was early. They had all gotten up before dawn to have an early breakfast. Dennis and the boys were in his cabin, busy curing furs for the soon-to-come Rendezvous. Every mountain man in the Rockies would be there, with French Canadian fur trading companies and a couple of American traders. It was the one time in the year when they saw more than a dozen people in the same place, and for two long weeks, there was constant partying with free drinks and food. Up to five hundred people would attend.

The trading companies maneuvered to buy the valuable cold-water beaver pelts. The French Canadians had the best supplies and the best prices, so the Americans had to wine and dine the rugged trappers to acquire the best furs. Beaver skin top hats were the rage back east in places like New York and Boston, not to mention the even larger markets in England, France, and Germany.

Angus sat on the edge of the porch feeding doves sunflower seeds as he sipped on his breakfast coffee. Steel sat at the porch table, tracing his finger under the words, and continued to read and mumble. He read a piece from the scriptures every morning when at home and not traveling. He read his Bible just as much for his spiritual education as to keep his mind sharp. Even though they would never admit it, they were aging, and the process was speeded up due to the harsh lifestyle and weather conditions.

"And what's wrong with time passing slow?" Angus asked. "That just means we're gonna live longer."

"You know what I mean," Rusty replied. "I reckon I'm just fiddle-footed, is all. I need some action in my life, and I need it quick, or I'm gonna be bored to death."

"Why, you wandered off all winter. That ain't enough, and you say you want it fast?" Angus asked. "Change your pants fast iffin ya want. But it'll be workin'. Your days are long because you sit around doin' nothing. You're as lazy as a sloth."

When Levi stepped onto the porch, the wood plank floor groaned. He had his pistols in his belt and a pack mule ready to go. When he dropped the reins, it pushed its head near the water trough and slurped.

"I reckon I'm gonna go out and get our month's meat." Levi smiled as he bounced on the balls of his feet. Obviously, he was itchy to get back out and on the hunt. "Maybe I can bag an elk or two. Maybe even a bear."

When Levi said he was going hunting, he assumed he would be going alone like always. That was when he was best. Most hunters didn't have the stealth Johnson had despite his size. He stood on the porch with his rifles in his hands, impatient to delve into the forest. It was his favorite place. He had hunted with a passion all his life, since he was a very young boy back in Southeastern Indiana. On some of the big hunts, even Rusty wasn't allowed to go, even though he was Levi's mentor. When it came to hunting, Johnson was the boss. That went for trapping too. When he was young back on the Ohio River, they didn't call him Trapper Boy for nothing.

Rusty knew he would just slow him down, so he let it slide. Johnson always came back with more game if he went solo. He claimed other people scared off the deer and elk. When he was alone, the animals seemed to come to him. It was something magical that he didn't want to pass on to anybody. It was a secret between Levi and Mother Nature.

Dahteste angrily slapped the tipi flap back and stormed across the yard to Rusty's cabin. She stood before her husband with her fists on her hips and her chin jutted out in defiance. It just dawned on him she would want to go too. As she caught him off guard, he stammered for a moment.

Levi racked his brain for what to say before he said, "Mornin', darlin'. I was just gonna go out and hunt up somethin' special to eat."

"You didn't even wake me up, Beaver," Dahteste

huffed in Crow. "Did it ever occur to you I might want to go too? You do remember you're married, don't you?"

"I thought we agreed you were only gonna speak English while here in the camp," Rusty said. "It'll do ya a world of good, young lady. Civilization is coming whether you like it or not, and if you speak English, you'll get by better."

Angus stopped feeding the doves, and Rusty pulled his eyes from Dahteste and stared at Levi. Both men had grins spread across their faces and were waiting to see how Johnson handled the new situation. They were always ready for a good laugh or a tasty bit of drama. The only sounds were from crickets as Levi's face went blank. He didn't know what to say.

Finally, Levi grumbled, "What are you two old bears lookin' at?"

Angus cackled and said, grinning, "Your face looks like somebody killed a beaver with a hammer."

"There ain't no saints in the animal kingdom—just breakfast and dinner," Levi retorted. He wanted to go alone, but he knew he couldn't tell Dahteste that she couldn't go.

"Remember, you're talking to a Crow war chief," Dahteste growled. Her mouth was a gash, and her eyes blazed in defiance.

"She's got spirit." Rusty chuckled. "You've gotta admit that. You married her, pilgrim. Now you have to deal with the wildcat."

Angus cackled again, and Rusty got a stitch. Dahteste's face was red as a tomato. Her eyes shot daggers at her husband, who'd been about to run off to hunt without telling her a thing. That was why she hadn't accepted any of her suitors back in the Crow camp. She refused to be treated like a common squaw. Levi Johnson was just about to find out he had married a honey badger. She didn't rank lower than just any man. Maybe Levi was a better fighter or hunter than she was, but he at least owed her the chance to find out. You never knew—she might outdo her new husband yet.

"Wait right here while I get my travel kit and gun. I won't be long," Dahteste said in English. Her eyes met Rusty's, and she winked, but her husband didn't see it. "You just watch. We'll come back with a fine catch."

When Dahteste disappeared into their tipi to put her travel kit together, Levi looked at Rusty and growled, "You know I don't like anybody goin' with me when I hunt. She'll just scare all the game away."

"What are ya tellin' us for?" Rusty laughed some more. "That's what you should be tellin' your wife. From where I'm sittin', I don't see you have a chance in Hades of goin' on your own. I thought you were more schooled in womenfolk than that."

"Why, I've never had the opportunity," Levi replied. "Dahteste is the first woman I've really been close to. We didn't have any neighbors back home in Indiana, and on the way west, I was focused on making a living and not gettin' scalped."

"Maybe you should have studied up on it a bit before ya got hitched," Angus smiled. "Iffin you'd have asked me, I'd have told ya all about it. I've had three Crow wives, so I'd say I'm an expert. Mind you, my women were ordinary Indian folk. Yours is a warrior chief. Now that I think about it, I doubt I'd know what to do were I in your shoes, but I ain't, and you are. Iffin you love the girl, you'll have to sway some, or you'll break just like a big, tall tree. Now you can't just run off and not say a word about it. I'm afraid you'll be taught a lesson today.

"You entered a partnership when you made the Fire of Five Woods in the wedding ceremony." Angus smiled. "If ya left her now, you would shame her, and Chief Hachta would be angry, no doubt. Then we'd all be in a mess. When you make that kind of decision, you should take your time to see if that's what you really want, but you two jumped into it with both feet. I know they say all that stuff about Cupid's arrow, but I have a hard time imaginin' a fat baby shootin' an arrow at anybody."

"Maybe it's just because you're ignorant as a piece of wood," Rusty growled. "Don't go and put fool notions in Levi's head. Marriage is sacred and a good thing. Give it a chance, boy. Maybe she'll turn out to be a better shot than you. I doubt you can use a bow and arrow as good as her. She'll be sharp as a tack and may just make the perfect huntin' partner. Dennis, Angus, and I have all failed in your eyes. She's your wife, boy. Give her the same chance you gave your friends. You watch how you'll please her. If you want to have a happy home, you're gonna have to maintain a happy wife."

When Dahteste finally showed up, everybody's eyes were fixed on the Crow woman. She was armed for bear. A quiver of arrows was strapped to her back with her longbow. Pistols protruded from her belt, and a big knife hung from her side. A sheathed long rifle was in her right hand.

"Come on, I'll lead," Dahteste said, chuckling as they made their way out of the compound. "I know Crow signs we leave for each other. If they see me, they won't bother us."

"And what if they're Blackfeet Indians?" Levi asked. "They ain't so friendly like the Crow."

"Then it's our duty to kill them as our tribe's enemies. The Blackfoot people have been our adversary since history was recorded," she said in her own language.

"I thought we were gonna speak English." Levi chuckled.

"We are on my tribe's land now, so we speak Crow. I will do as promised when we are in the compound and speak only English. It isn't easy, but I will succeed. You didn't marry a stupid woman, Levi." She smiled while mischief danced in her eyes.

When they got to the hunting grounds, they dropped down off their horses and led them by their leads. Neither he nor she made a sound as they crept toward a waterhole that only Levi knew about. When they arrived, two white-tailed deer slurped from the still water, refreshing themselves. Suddenly, they popped their heads up with their eyes stretched wide. They bounded away from the danger even though Dahteste and Levi were sure they hadn't startled them. It was something else that had made them run. He was itching to pull the trigger as he scoured as far as he could see.

Dahteste sniffed the air and frowned. She looked at Beaver, and with her lips, she silently mouthed, "Grizzly bear."

Hackles rose on the mountain man's neck. "Where?" he whispered.

She sniffed again, looked past her husband, and pointed and said, "He's right behind you."

Both put their guns to their shoulders, and the bear charged. Levi Beaver Johnson was calm, cool, and collected as he took a bead. He pulled the trigger, and the hammer struck the flint. A spark appeared, but the gun didn't shoot.

"Misfire!" Levi shouted.

A shot rang out as smoke trailed out of Dahteste's barrel. The bullet hit the bear in the chest, stopping it in its tracks, but it didn't go down. It swatted at the chunk of lead like it was a pesky fly. Blood poured from its mouth, but it wasn't out of fight yet. It screamed a sound neither the Crow woman nor the mountain man had ever heard before. It was like it came from the bowels of hell.

The Crow warrior turned for a tree, and Levi yelled, "Don't you dare climb up there, or he'll get cha for sure! There's cover in that cave over there. We've got to try to make it."

Johnson pulled both pistols, and the guns bucked in his hands. He aimed for the animal's eyes, but he missed with it shaking its head and swatting at the pain with its paws.

"Come on, run!" Levi shouted, yanking Dahteste's arm as they broke into a dead run.

Nothing but fear could move two people so fast. Their arms pumped up and down like steam engine pistons. Levi's heart redlined, and they hit the halfway mark. He took a chance and looked back. The bear was just getting its bearings again, and it locked eyes with the hunter. It charged again. Heat waves could be seen in the distance as the spring sun hammered down. Finally, they rushed from the sunlight into the dark of the smelly cavern. They crawled into the cave ankle-deep in musky water. Now wouldn't be the time to take a tumble. They suddenly found themselves in a cool, dark, musky-smelling cave. It was dark, creepy, and clammy. They had no idea how deep it was. Layers of filmy water stood in puddles. Their moccasins were soaked. They went into a crouch as their hearts ricocheted against their ribs. Rats, leeches, and spiders crawled silently in the dark. The floor of the cave was covered with moss.

"Oh, no! This is the bear's cave," Levi said as he gobbled air.

They had to stop briefly, or their hearts would burst. Still, their lungs burned as they tried to gobble enough air.

"He'll follow us in here if it's his den," Dahteste said with eyes spread wide. "The smell of bear is strong. I think I see a hint of light at the other end."

"COME ON!" Levi said urgently.

He nearly dragged his wife off her feet as they raced for the other end of the tunnel. They ducked lower, picking up their pace again, running for their lives.

Their hearts picked up when they heard rushing water. When they came to the end of the tunnel, it opened to a cliff with a roaring river below them. Dahteste and Levi locked eyes, then they looked back. They could hear the bear. Now he was making a beeline for the hunters and was moving fast. He knew his way in the dark, so the cave must be his.

"Hold on tight to your rifle, darlin'!" Levi shouted. "We're gonna have to jump." It was a twenty-foot drop. His words reverberated off the canyon walls.

It was like landing on hard sand and freezing cold when they hit the water. The current instantly swept them away. Both looked up at the cave. The grizzly bear was watching them disappear as it looked down on the fleeing prey. The hunters had become the hunted before they knew it but had managed to escape.

They were swept down the carved-out, twisting river and into the swirling spray until it widened, and the whitewater was replaced with ripples. Finally, their feet could touch the ground. They scurried up the bank, slipping on the slick, wet, moss-covered bottom until they reached the water's edge. Levi and his wife pawed their way up the embankment, groping for weeds and rocks—anything that might hold their weight as they crawled out of the water, up the bank, and rolled onto soft grass under the shade of lines of trees all along the riverbank.

Their hearts were in a sprint, and their thoughts were jumbled and confused from the rag doll shaking the rapids had given them. Levi checked his powder horn and discovered his powder was wet. It was the same with Dahteste. The fall had worked the plugs loose, and water had gotten in.

"Now we've only got our bow and arrows to defend ourselves," Levi said as he huffed, slowly recovering his breath and forcing his heart to slow down. Again, the married couple locked eyes, and they began to laugh.

"That was close." Dahteste giggled. It was nervous laughter—the kind that followed a narrow escape with one's life.

"I think it's time to go home," Levi said.

UNSEEN ENEMIES

THE CAPTAIN RODE POINT WITH THE REINS AND A PISTOL in his hand. The mustang was rugged and surefooted, even on the treacherous trail. They silently rode down steep paths barely visible as they stood in their stirrups, and then across green valleys, but now they saw no more buffalo. This was too close to the Indian hunters. The buffalo knew where to go to graze in peace—at least until the buffalo hunters showed.

Now, the skins stank on the backs of the mules, and hundreds of flies buzzed around them. The mules' ears twitched, and their tails swatted, constantly failing to shoo them away. Virgil had slipped his bandana over his mouth and nose to keep them from lighting and crawling in, but still, they tried to land on his eyes. Riding drag, he was behind all the stink, blood, skin, and dust.

Flocks of crows flew from tree to tree as they chased the riders, perching on the limbs like pallbearers. Virgil rode drag because he was the best shot and had the most experience after Levi. Even though now he was doing something he hadn't done since he was a young man: he was running for his life. It had been many years since he had this feeling, and it wasn't welcome. Still, all four raced down the mountain as quickly as possible with the loaded-down mules. They were slowing them down, but they carried what they had come to the mountains to acquire: hundreds of dollars in buffalo hides.

"If we're caught, we'll be between the devil and the deep-blue sky," the captain said as he looked back at the men closely following.

The captain's blood began to race in anticipation, with vindication only a few days away. They had been fleeing for seven days and had seen no sign of the Crow so far. But somehow, the West Point officer knew they were coming. It was just a matter of time. He watched as the wall of the buffalo hunter's conviction cracked like an iceberg. At first, it showed little flaws, but soon their determination cracked like a china plate under a hammer.

Bud Guns cleared his throat. The large lump of Adam's apple was visible when he swallowed—it bobbed up and down. Clinch West's eyes were popping out of his head. Only Virgil took it all in stride. He had been in similar situations and had obviously survived. The captain was glad one of the three was levelheaded and had the grit it took to do the job.

The other two were great shots but didn't have the stuff it took to fight Indians. They weren't even very good at handling the wilderness. But they had come here to do a job they were very good at. He had a sneaking suspicion that his new friend, Virgil Lovejoy, had experienced as bad, if not worse.

The sad truth started to sink in. The captain had considered side-kicking up with Virgil, but he didn't want the extra baggage that Bud and Clinch would bring. Both men seemed honest enough, but West was too nervous, and Bud was simply too dumb. Traveling with them would be a burden and maybe a hindrance. They might even get a man killed. He had a gut feeling about Virgil, and despite all their apparent differences, he felt they had some things in common. He could almost see what it was, but it eluded him in a distant fog. Still, he knew Virgil was of similar beliefs.

Clinch West was an ex-Army man who had never been posted on the Indian frontier forts. The captain could see it in his eyes; this was all new to him. Then there was Bud Guns. He was always on the defensive because he was more aware than most thought that he was as dumb as mud. He tried to fake his way through life, acting like he wasn't what he was, but the captain saw right through his facade.

The captain pushed these thoughts aside and focused on the task at hand. First, they had to get out of the mountains before the Crow warriors found them, and find them they would if they didn't make haste. He did not doubt their tracking skills. He knew that if the Crow warriors caught up with them, there would be a clamorous battle, and he had no idea what the outcome would be. That all depended on how many warrior braves came after them. He hoped that with the distance, some would tire of the chase and drop off and go home.

Then again, he knew wishful thinking was dangerous when such a skilled opponent chased you in uncertain numbers on unknown land. It was better to always consider the worst at every corner. As they traveled, he constantly spotted the best locations to fight from. The captain always looked for high ground and a clear field of fire. That could make all the difference. He only hoped that if and when they caught up, it would be on his terms and in a place he could choose and defend.

He couldn't say for sure, but he felt they should be down from the mountain in five to seven days if they could keep up their fast pace. Only Bud Guns was struggling to keep up with the rest. The five to seven days was pretty much a guess, as the captain couldn't remember riding up the mountain in the first place. He wondered if he'd been alone or if he had lost an entire patrol. Suppose he had; then where were the signs of their presence? He hadn't seen shoed horse tracks since he found himself on the cliff horseless.

They hoofed their way down and scrambled over the rocks. For the captain, there was only one place to go, where he felt at home and knew nobody would find him. This was something he knew deep inside, but for the life of him, he couldn't remember where, or even what, it was. Still, he knew it was there. Was this the place he was looking for when his horse fell to its death? Or was it somewhere near the frontier forts of Kansas, or maybe even where he came from? He knew he wasn't born in this part of the country, but still, he didn't know where it was.

The officer was aware of his education even though he didn't know where he studied. He could tell by how his mind worked when compared to Bud and Clinch or even Virgil, who was light years smarter than his two helpers. The captain wondered what Lovejoy's plans were after he sold the hides and paid off his shooters.

This was a dangerous country to travel alone, and it was always good to have a guard at night and an extra pair of eyes.

He clearly knew how to survive in the wilderness, and he could kill a man if pressed. This was no country for the weak of heart, especially with several hostile Indian tribes fighting for the wild game and land. They not only fought the European intruders but each other too. The Plains Indians were a warrior tribe.

As the day waned and the light began to soften, the captain located a defensive position. He knew that darkness came as suddenly as a spark when the sun dropped behind the mountain peaks towering over them. They had to move quickly to unload the mules, brush the animals down, and get them fed. They had watered them shortly before stopping. The captain couldn't risk being on low ground near a stream at night. It would leave them open to an attack.

The hill he chose was nearly barren. At the top were clusters of rocks. They made their camp nestled inside two boulders. There, they finally chanced making a small fire before it was dark. It was nearing dusk, so what little smoke the fire produced was hidden in shadows, and it wasn't dark enough for anyone to see the fire itself.

Bud pulled out some bacon to fry over an iron rod. He was famished, and the coffee didn't fulfill his needs. His mouth watered at the anticipated taste. Drool dripped down the edge of his mouth and chin.

"Don't you even think about putting that bacon on to fry," the captain demanded. "Heck, I can smell freshly fried bacon two hundred yards away. We're already taking our chances with the coffee. Here, chew on this hard tack. It's going to have to do for now. I doubt we'll be able to make a proper fire and a real meal until we get out of the mountains."

They selected the best cover to sleep while two men stayed awake to watch their surroundings. The sun fell off the end of the world. Momentarily, the sky was on fire with a prism of light, then they were suddenly plunged into darkness.

"Clinch, you and Bud take the first watch. After four hours, wake us up, and the captain and me will take the night owl shift. That's when it's more likely for hostiles to strike. Ain't that right, sir?"

"That sure sounds about right to me, even if I don't remember why. Yeah, the Indians will attack at dawn or maybe even a little earlier if they're still there. We don't want to let our guard down, but we're getting pretty close to our objective. I'm beginning to believe we might have outrun them."

"Maybe they did like you said before," Bud said. "You know, dropping off because they're bored and tired out. That sounds about right to me." He twisted the ends of his massive mustache.

Later that night, the first sliver of the moon appeared. It was just enough to make everything silvery and create shadows where the enemy could hide.

As soon as Clinch woke the captain and Virgil, he and Bud immediately dropped off into a deep sleep. Both men snored softly as the guards took over their jobs and scoured their position for the enemy. Virgil and the captain sat leaning against each other's backs. Each man kept watch on one hundred and eighty degrees. Nobody was allowed to go out and tend to their personals. It was just too dangerous alone at night.

"Do you think they're still chasing us after a week, Captain?" Virgil whispered.

"I don't have a bad feeling in my gut, so my guess is they gave up and headed back home," the captain said. "It's dangerous out here for the Crow Indians too. There'll be Blackfeet snooping around here looking for their lifelong enemies."

That night, the two new friends whispered through the early morning hours. By first light, they knew a bit more about each other. Virgil shared that he was an enslaved person in Alabama when he was a young man. He had been lucky because his original owner sold him after three escapes. But they caught him each time. There were too many White men looking for Negros roaming the southern countryside, acting like they were free.

Finally, the brown man was sold to the aging Englishman Fitzgerald Worstshire III. When he died, he left Virgil Lovejoy in his will. He wasn't to be inherited by his many children as expected, but Worstshire had granted him his freedom along with all his enslaved people. They were all declared free men and women. Virgil had served his last owner well because he was a fair man—or as far as an enslaver could be. Lovejoy had traveled west to the frontier forts. The farther west he went, the safer he felt, and he finally arrived in Montana. There, he discovered his knack for guns and rifles, and he trapped and hunted for a living, much like Will Forrester did with the Army when he first set out.

Of course, the only insight Virgil got out of the captain was his attitude. He noticed that the captain acted like he was just as whole as any man, even though he was missing an arm. He was so full of energy it vibrated into Lovejoy's awareness. He could tell he was sizing him up despite the odd pair of companions they made. He wondered where they would go if they did sidekick up.

The sun came up in the east as the sliver of moon could still be seen in the western sky. It hung as if on a string before a field of blue sky. The sun's rays shot out from behind the peaks, making a spectacle of a new dawn. Both men tore their eyes away from the sections they were guarding. They had made it through the night. Before it got fully light, Virgil made up coffee and frying pan biscuits. The captain caved in after such a quiet night and allowed them to fry some bacon. As soon as the sizzling aroma reached Bud's nose, he blinked and stretched, then sat up and rubbed his eyes with his fists. A smile spread across his austere face. Clinch West was right behind him. Mouths watered as they impatiently waited.

Bud was just reaching for a second biscuit when the lance came sailing in. The flint head pierced his chest and ran halfway through his body. He was startled, and his eyes popped wide as he looked down. He had the biscuit halfway to his mouth, but when he opened it, blood poured out. The second spear pierced Clinch's neck and nearly took his head off. He was killed instantly. The strange thing was they saw and heard nobody, no matter how hard they strained their eyes and ears. But the captain knew the lances were Crow. They had found them, after all.

Both survivors ducked low behind the boulders, so they weren't another target for another spear, arrow, or gun. Both men's faces glistened with sweat as they clenched their pistols.

"I figure it's just a matter of time now," Virgil said. "If we don't get out of this, it was mighty nice knowin' you, Captain, and I'm sorry you never discovered who you were."

"Think positive, Virgil," the captain said. "It could be a pair of warriors who got lucky because we got lax and thought we were safe. I should have known better."

"Don't put all the blame on yourself, pilgrim," Virgil said. "I brought those two youngins up here, so I'm as much to blame as anybody. Anyway, ponderin' on hindsight is a waste of time."

Even though both men were sure the Crow warriors' attack was imminent, they waited the entire day and no one showed—not a single Indian. Yet, both men knew there was at least one warrior brave out there. They sat hidden behind the boulder the entire day with their guns laid out before them for when the attack eventually came. They knew it would. Otherwise, nothing made any sense.

The sun set on the horizon, leaving the survivors puzzled. Then again, Indians had strange ways. Maybe they thought that with two dead, the score was even. But that didn't explain why they didn't take the buffalo hides. Maybe the enemy didn't want them, but that made even less sense.

When the sun neared the horizon, the captain said, "We've got to get out of here under cover of darkness. Come on and help me pack the mules."

"What do we do with Clinch and Bud's horses?" Virgil asked.

"We can take them with us," the captain said. "A couple of spare horses will come in handy in case we lose the ones we're riding. I know it's a hell of a time to think about the dead, but it rubs me wrong to leave those two young men there to be eaten by the vultures. Before we leave, we can dig a grave each and still get away while it's dark."

"These boys had kin folk somewhere, but I can't remember where it was," Virgil fretted. "It's a doggone shame they had to lose their lives."

"At least they went quick," the captain replied, pushing his foot on the shovel and the first rung to hell. "This feels so familiar. I just know I've buried my soldiers just like we're burying Guns and West."

FAMILIAR FACES

ONCE THEY HAD BURIED BUD AND CLINCH, THEY FINISHED packing the mules and saddled the horses. There wasn't even time to make crosses to mark the graves. Before they left, Virgil read a few passages from his worn and tattered Bible. He must have memorized them because, although he stared at his open book and spoke the words with conviction and confidence, he couldn't see the letters. The small amount of light provided by the sliver of the moon and the twinkling blanket of stars wasn't enough.

The captain used Clinch's saddle, and Bud's was tied to the last mule. The dead men's horses ran behind the riders on string leads. Dust curled behind the small party of travelers. Now they knew they had been located. All they could do was continue to flee and hope for the best. So far, they hadn't even seen their pursuers.

They picked their way through the forest, careful not to slip in the dark and end up plunging down the side of a mountain. Both Virgil and the captain looked over their shoulder all day. That was where mister paranoia was permanently perched. As their numbers dwindled, they saw they might not make it down even though it was only a few days more—especially if they maintained the current neck-breaking pace.

They continued to ride as quickly as they could without becoming reckless. Now they felt if one thing didn't kill them, something else would. Neither man had forgotten all the perilous animals that also populate the mountains. There was danger on all sides. All the time, the captain looked for tracks, but he found none. There wasn't a trace of the enemy, but he still felt they might be following. A man just never knew what went through a Crow warrior's mind. It was pretty much a mystery to the people from back east.

They rode through the day, looking back so often that their necks ached. Paranoia had burrowed deep into their souls, and now they didn't even trust their own eyes.

"I may be seein' things, but that looks like some smoke down there in the next valley," Virgil said in a hushed voice. He pointed. "Over there on the side of the mountain."

Three steady trails of smoke and one smaller one squirreled into the light blue canvas. There wasn't a cloud in the sky.

"I hope it isn't more Indians," the captain said. "I feel like we're going from the skillet to the frying pan. All we need now is to run into a Blackfoot camp."

"What choice do we have, Captain?" Virgil asked. "You saw how fast they killed Bud and Clinch. I don't fancy spending my days buried here in the mountains. Whatcha say, sir? Shall we go have a look-see?"

"I guess we don't have much to lose or much

choice," the captain replied. "It's that or spend another evening alone, and we might not make it through the night this time. I just hope these are folks like you and me and not hostiles."

As soon as they rode out of the dense forest, they came to a stretch of cleared land and a zigzag fence—one by one, the horses, riders, and mules walked to the edge of a compound. Virgil stood in the stirrups and looked for the gate. Luckily, it was open. He led horses and mules, as did the second rider. Three cabins appeared before their eyes, and strangely enough, a tipi stood between the last two dwellings. A half dozen White men with long hair and great beards sat on the porch. An old fellow sat on the edge with his legs dangling.

"Howdy, ma'am, ladies," the amiable rider said as he walked his horse toward the porch and tipped his hat.

A string of loaded mules followed, and another rider rode drag, but he was hard to see in the dust kicked up by a dozen animals. "You the owner?" Virgil asked the mountain man sitting on the porch.

"That be me—Rusty Steel's the name, and Angus McFarlin here is my trappin' partner," the long-haired mountain man replied, nodding. "And you...?" He still couldn't see the face of the rider behind him.

"We just lost two men this very morning, or we wouldn't impose on your privacy, sir," the brown man said. "The captain says Crow Indians is who killed my two employees. As you can see from the hides, we're buffalo hunters. But we come from way up in the mountains. There ain't even any Indians up there, but somehow the buffalo find the place. My name is Virgil

Lovejoy, and back there's the captain." Virgil politely smiled and tipped his hat.

Finally, the captain wheeled his horse onto the familiar trail. This was the last place he had been before he left on a trip and lost his memory. He didn't know how he knew, but he did.

The mountain men and the two Crow women heard the beating of hooves. When the captain came into sight, he raced toward the wooden zigzag fence. The rider leaned toward the jump as the horse's graceful muscles bunched in his hind legs. When he leaped, he cleared the fence. The graceful image of the captain on his horse making the jump into the mountain men's compound was frozen for a second in the minds of the people watching.

It landed on its forelegs without missing a stride, and he pulled up to a sliding stop with questioning eyes. He didn't recognize anybody there, but still, there was something familiar in the voice of the man he'd heard talk, the one who said he was Rusty Steel. They locked eyes, and the captain saw the recognition in the mountain man's stare. Then it changed to a puzzled one.

"It's good to see some European folks for a change," the captain said, unsure of himself.

He looked at the party of trappers and Indian women without the slightest hint of recognition. Just hearing Forrester's voice, Levi's blood instantly heated, but he acted like he didn't recognize his friend. He racked his brain for what to say. He and his wife both waited with a bit of anxiousness for him to answer. They could see him go over it in his mind. Dahteste hadn't missed it when he said Crow warriors killed two of their party. She wondered what happened to the captain. He didn't act like the same man.

Levi and Dahteste's eyes ran to each other as soon as they saw the captain. Forrester instantly saw something between them, but even his best friend Levi was unrecognizable to him. He sat on his horse, leaning on the pommel as he stared and tried to remember, but nothing came. The captain felt he had done his fair share of good. It was just something he knew inside. Now, he felt like he had been drifting ever since. It crossed his mind that he was somehow given a second chance. But no matter how hard he tried to remember, he found nothing familiar in their faces or even the cabins before him. All he had was a gut feeling he had been here before.

"Howdy, ladies, gentlemen. I'm the captain."

Everybody there just stood and gawked at Forrester with their mouths hanging to their chins. They didn't know what to say, but he clearly didn't recognize anybody.

"Captain what?" Levi asked. He looked confused.

"Don't pay the captain no mind," Virgil said, smiling. "He's as good a man as I've ever known, so don't take offense. Why, I found 'im up in the highest part of the Rockies while I was hunting buffs with my two men, may they rest in peace. He'd been thrown by his horse, or at least that's what we figured. The animal must have fallen off the narrow trail into the gorge a few hundred feet below. There ain't no way it survived, and even if we could have gotten down there to recover his things, we'd have never been able to climb back out. We'd have to have wings to climb down there and get out again.

Anyway, the captain hit his head, and he has what folks back east call amnesia."

"You don't have to tell everybody my life's story, Virgil," the captain barked. Everybody there looked at him like they knew him. His mind began to spin out of control, and he grabbed the saddle horn to keep from falling off his horse.

"That must have been your white stallion that died," Rusty said. "You really don't remember us, do ya, Captain Forrester? That's right, your name is Will Forrester, and this big fella sitting right here is your best friend, Levi Johnson."

The captain sat in the saddle, frozen like ice. It hit him like a ton of bricks when it came—he didn't know these people. He looked at Virgil for help, but Lovejoy looked back at his new friend with sad eyes.

"Did I live here? And you say my name is Will Forrester? What in the world am I doing living up here when I'm clearly an Army captain?"

"Well, pard, it's a long story," Levi said. "Step down and take a load off. I reckon you don't remember my wife either. This here is my darlin' Dahteste. She's a Crow war chief."

It brought hazy memories to mind when Levi spoke, but Will couldn't quite make them out. Still, the part of his brain that held memories had a dark veil over it.

The captain stopped in midstride. The Crow were the people who had killed Bud and Clinch. He suddenly felt unsure of himself. His eyes locked with Virgil's, and their smiles changed to no more than gashes, and their eyes narrowed.

"You say she's a Crow war chief?" Captain Forrester asked. "It was Crow that killed the two youngsters."

Virgil and Forrester were so shocked they didn't see everybody's eyes turn to the end of the compound. On a magnificent pony rode a man with long hair decorated with beads and brads. He wore a fancy headdress and a red buckskin shirt. Pistols protruded from his belt, and a bow hung from his back along with a quiver of arrows. The captain immediately recognized the lance. It was the same one that killed Bud Guns.

Captain Forrester followed their eyes to the man waking his horse into the compound. The Indian warrior acted like he owned the place and was completely alone. Had this lone man attacked them and killed half their hunting party?

"I'm gonna rip the bark right off your skin," Forrester growled like a rabid dog. His eyes narrowed, and he stared at the Crow Indian.

"Whoa, whoa, whoa, now!" Rusty yelled. "What in the world is goin' on with you two? You act like you're enemies."

"Woe to those that call evil good and good evil," Chief Hachta hissed. He sounded like a viper.

"Hold on a dad-gummed minute," Angus ordered. "Get down off them horses right now, and let's all have a coffee and a smoke before we say another word. What in the world has gotten into you two?"

"This Indian killed our friends," Forrester growled.

"What's wrong with the captain, Mr. Lovejoy?" Rusty asked.

"He can't remember who he is," Virgil replied. "Ain't that right, Captain?"

Forrester gave his friend a dirty look, but still, defiance was etched on his face—that and puzzlement. It was all so confusing he was having a hard time getting out a word. It was impossible for him to wrap his mind around what was happening.

BROKEN RELATIONS

DESPITE HACHTA BEING A CROW CHIEF, HE SAW THE wisdom in what Angus McFarlin had to say and followed his suggestion. He kicked his leg over his horse's neck and slid off the animal's back. He still held the long lance in his hand. There was blood on the tip, and hair hung from the end. Virgil couldn't take his eyes off Bud Guns's bright red scalp hanging from the flint spearhead.

The men sat at the porch table. Now, protocol was paramount. Angus knew enough about living with the Crow to know he could reason with such a chief as Hachta. He was famous all over these mountains. Then again, so were some of the mountain men.

Rusty broke out a fresh twist of tobacco while Angus made a gallon pot of coffee. Soon, the aromas floated on puffs of air. Steel looked from one angry man to the other. Virgil seemed to have resigned himself to follow whatever path the captain chose. He was tired of running. He felt he had run enough for a lifetime.

They stuffed their ceramic and corncob pipes with

tobacco, and soon, smoke floated around their heads. Both men were beginning to simmer down.

"This here is Crow Chief Hachta," Rusty started. "He and his people own everything as far as the eye can see. They've been kind enough to let us live here on the mountain. In exchange, we provide them with the occasional rifle and steel tools. We also help them sell their beaver pelts come time for the Rendezvous. That's why two of your men died for trespassin' on Crow land and stealin' their buffalo. Y'all be lucky you didn't lose your lives too. I reckon the chief recognized Will right off, but his family has a dark past in the calvary, so it was normal for the Hachta to think the worst."

"When you and I came here, we were searching for a new life away from people," Levi said. "I wanted to be a mountain man, and you were runnin' away from your past, my friend. This man you wanna kill is the person that allowed us to live here. I believe that's why you're still breathin'. You and your new friend Virgil there. Well, Mr. Lovejoy, a friend of the captain is a friend of mine, so you make yourself at home."

That struck a sore spot inside the captain. It all fit with what Levi and Rusty had told him earlier. Now, he was more confused than ever. His life had plunged into chaos, and he couldn't remember who he was. He wanted to kill a man who allowed him to live on his land and eat his game. He was starting to see the problem but still didn't remember anything.

"I reckon we were wrong about you, Chief," Captain Forrester said. "Was it you all on your own out there?"

"Why would I need more men if you were only four?" Chief Hachta asked arrogantly. "You can keep the buffalo skins you stole from my people. You have already paid too much. But don't come back to our mountains to hunt buffalo. This we won't permit."

"That's mighty kind of ya, Chief," Virgil said. "It was big of ya not to kill us all, too, and I thank ya kindly. You sure do speak good English for an Indian."

"It is better to know all you can about your enemies," Hachta said. "If I can't understand what you say, how can I defeat you?"

Captain Forrester and Virgil stayed on for a week to rest up, so everybody could tell him all the stories they knew about his past. He wanted desperately to know more about his old self. When things started to sink in, Forrester became more and more confused. It was impossible to fathom all that they had told him. Levi had gone through the whole story from when they met up in Kansas at the frontier forts. As he described their battles with Comanche warriors, it struck a nerve. That was why he hadn't been worried about the young Crow warriors. Still, after an entire afternoon of hearing his life's story, he didn't remember a thing. He didn't even understand how they seemed to feel about him because he felt nothing for them. They were all strangers to him. The only familiar one was his sidekick, Virgil Lovejoy. He was the only man there he trusted.

Rusty and Levi took turns telling their story of West Point Captain William Forrester of the United States Calvary. Still, the officer felt the same emptiness he had felt since he woke up several days before. For him, his life started just over a week ago, and everything else before that was nothing to him. When he searched in his mind, all he found were dark shadows. Voices had a small ring of memory, but the faces he was seeing didn't mean anything. It was like he'd never seen them before. It was all gone and forgotten.

After just a week with people he didn't recognize, he was itching to get going. Virgil had already been prepared to head out for a couple of days.

The following day, they had the mules loaded with hides, and the horses were saddled.

"I guess we'll see each other again at the Rendezvous, won't we?" Forrester asked.

"I'd like that just fine," Levi said. "I'll be lookin' forward to it."

The riders, horses, and mules slowly snaked out of the compound and began the ride down the rest of the trail. Now they had Hachta's word that no more Crow would bother them. Still, they had to worry about the Blackfeet, but there was always some danger or another in the wilderness in the Rocky Mountains.

Levi and Dahteste sat and swang back and forth on the porch glider. Johnson stared off into space wondering how such a thing could happen. Bob and Sam were pitching pennies against the sunny side of the cabin. Rusty sat at the table reading a year-old newspaper while Angus fed sunflower seeds to the doves

A Look at Book Six:
Rendezvous: A Western Double

Every man meets his reckoning on the trail west.

Rendezvous

Levi Johnson, his Crow wife Dahteste, and the mountain men ride down from the Rockies for the annual Rendezvous. With pelts to trade and changes brewing, Rusty Steel leads the way —hoping to cross paths with old friends. But one is missing: Captain Will Forrester, lost to the wilderness and his own broken memory.

As the group heads for the gathering, so do others—buffalo hunters, drifters, and dangerous men with secrets to hide. Not everyone is there to trade, and not all will make it back alive.

Mayhem on the Oregon Trail

Just as the mountain men regroup, tragedy strikes. Yosemite Bob is murdered by the feuding Squirrel clan, and a deadly pursuit begins. But justice grows complicated when the killers travel with a wagon train full of women and children—and more mountain men fall in the fight.

Meanwhile, Sheriff Joseph Walker is leading a group of missionaries west but loses his scouts on the trail. Desperate, he rides to the Rendezvous for help. He finds Levi, Rusty, and Will—men shaped by the land, the warpath, and the weight of hard choices.

AVAILABLE NOVEMBER 2025

ABOUT THE AUTHOR

Ash Lingam was born and raised in Southern Ohio, not far from the mighty Ohio River. He had somewhat of an isolated upbringing on a family farm with his sisters. His best friends were his horse, Sugar, and his grandfather.

Born in 1886, the family patriarch grew crops, raised cattle, and doted on the young boy. At his grandfather's side, Ash learned about livestock and firearms at an early age. His grandad carried an old Colt with him at all times. It helped spawn a young boy's dreams of yesteryear.

Ash was only eight years old when his grandad taught him how to trap muskrats to prevent them from draining the farm's ponds. He gave him a double-barreled shotgun at twelve and taught him how to hunt to put food on the table.

It wasn't long before Ash was breaking horses. His spirited Tennessee Walker never allowed any other rider on her back. Together, they searched through the plowed fields in the spring, looking for Miami Indian arrowheads to add to his grandfather's ample collection.

Ash's family was among the early settlers in pre-

Revolutionary America. He has traced his lineage back to around 1746 when his ancestors immigrated from Europe to the aspiring American Colonies.

A retired marketing executive, Ash devotes his spare time to training police dogs and writing novels. He has found his niche in the Western, historical fiction, and adventure genres. With his vast vault of experience, he never runs out of sources for new stories. He has lived in eleven different countries and worked in a total of forty-six to date, Ash has written approximately 130 novels, short stories, and poems. More than one hundred of his eclectic titles help the American frontier come alive for his readers.

https://www.ashlingam.com/
Join the Lawless Waters Western Readers & Writers
Facebook Group